THE LOVED
AND THE UNLOVED

FRANÇOIS MAURIAC

THE LOVED
AND
THE UNLOVED

TRANSLATED BY
GERARD HOPKINS

NEW YORK
PELLEGRINI & CUDAHY

Manufactured in the United States of America

Léonora Dori—more commonly known as Galigaï—was the wife of Concini, the favorite of Marie de Médicis. She was involved in the disgrace of her husband, and burned as a witch in 1617. When asked by her judges what magic she had employed in order to dominate the mind of Marie de Médicis, she replied: "My only magic was that to be found in the power of the strong-minded over the weak."

Contents

THE LOVED
AND THE UNLOVED

1

"YOU turned round twice!"

Marie raised one shoulder in a shrug.

"She didn't really turn round, Madame Agathe, did she?"

The noise of the bells relieved the governess from the need of answering. The Dubernet couple moved easily among the various groups, with a smile for all, but without involving themselves with any. It was said in Dorthe that no one could come out of church after High Mass with such an air as Julia Dubernet, that no one knew better how to give to each her due—and no more. She was a thin woman, but her protuberant stomach gave her a look of royalty. There had been hints—a growth, perhaps?

"Madame Mongie is waving to us," said Marie.

"Don't stop!" her mother hissed at her through clenched teeth, "they're with the Arbibats, and I have no wish to be introduced to the Arbibats!"

The Dubernet ladies hurried across the Place, under the fierce sun. It was concave in shape, and seemed to sag under its weight of centuries. The houses—every shutter was closed as though an enemy were expected to march in at any moment—stood shoulder to shoulder each supporting the other against the threat of imminent collapse. Flies were buzzing round the scattered garbage. In the middle of the open space, in full view of everybody, three dogs were nosing round a motionless bitch.

At last they reached the arcade. How blessed the shade was after the passage through that fiery furnace! Only one shop was open, Caliot's, the confectioner's. As always on Sundays, Marie's mind was set on the éclair which she regularly ate—"just as luncheon is almost on the table!" her mother was in the habit of complaining. But not to-day.

"We mustn't stop. Madame Agathe can fetch the tart. If the Arbibats saw us going into Caliot's, they'd make a beeline for us, and we should be caught. I wonder if you'd very much mind calling in for the tart, Madame Agathe?"

The governess had moved away from them. Camblanes though she was, she seemed all eagerness to oblige. Madame Dubernet never gave an order without remembering that this inferior was, by birth, a Camblanes, without feeling slightly flattered, vaguely embarrassed, and definitely compassionate. She watched Madame Agathe walking away, took note of the skinny neck emerging from a creased blouse, of the thin back-hair, of the summer frock which concealed nothing: "Bones like a bird's

. . . but there's something about breeding . . . you can't get away from that!"

They slipped into the hall. The walls showed great stains of damp. On the ground floor was the range of offices which served no purpose now that Armand Dubernet had given up "the banking." He had kept it on only so as to give himself something to do, said Madame Dubernet. "Thank God," she would add, "he has enough to live on without being obliged to work!" He had retired when those great sharks, the Credit Houses, had splashed into the calm waters where small savings could pile up undisturbed. His wife's admiration was based upon the solid foundation of that single fact—he had not allowed himself to be swallowed up by the Credit Houses!

Dark though the staircase was, it was like emerging from the glare of noon to pass from the landing into the first-floor rooms, where the white loose-covers were the only visible landmarks. Both the old owl and the little owl were accustomed to the dim obscurity. Flies and sunlight are the sworn enemies of those who live in Dorthe, and, from Spring onwards, in self-defense, condemn themselves to live in a world of artificial dusk.

In the middle of the drawing room, close to a pedestal-table, Armand Dubernet sat slumped in a chair. A single pencil-thread of blinding brilliance, in which innumerable specks of dust were dancing, struck across the room and caught his skull.

"Mass seems to have taken a long time to-day!"

"It mightn't have seemed so if you had been there!"

He lifted one shoulder in a shrug, just as his daughter had done a few minutes earlier. He must say something —it didn't much matter what—so as to stop Julia from starting off on her favorite subject—the danger of sudden death—and quoting the example of Larrier, the butcher, who had always told the curé that he would call him in before it was too late, and had been carried off in the very moment of flagrant sin . . . Hurriedly he asked whether there had been many people in church. Marie had sat down as far as possible from him. Julia Dubernet, standing in front of the mirror over the chimney-piece, was drawing two long pins from her hat and her "bun" of hair.

"Would you believe it, when we came out the Mongies were talking to the Arbibats! It was extremely tiresome, because of course I had to bow to the Mongies, and I expect the Arbibats thought I meant to include them!"

"Anything nice at Caliot's?"

"We didn't go in, because of the Arbibats. But Madame Agathe is fetching the tart."

"But how about your éclair, my pet, your famous luncheon's-almost-on-the-table éclair?"

His voice changed, grew softer, when he addressed his daughter.

"Don't speak to her! She turned round twice!"

The girl was on the brink of tears. She said: "To hear you talk, one might think it was a crime to turn one's head in church!"

"Don't play the hypocrite! You know perfectly well what it means when you turn your head in one particular direction! Everyone's talking about it at this very moment, you can be quite sure of that!"

Monsieur Dubernet asked a question: "Was *he* there?"

"Of course he was—with the inseparable Plassac!"

The girl, who had gone to the window and was pressing her forehead to the glass, though there was nothing to be seen except the reflection of her own dark-complexioned face, burst out sobbing and made for the door.

"That's done it!" grumbled Monsieur Dubernet: "lunch'll be ruined! I suppose you realize we're having prawns?"

"So much the worse for your bladder."

"About the child—you're making a mountain out of a molehill, you know."

"You really regard it as a molehill?"

"After all, the boy *is* Salone's son . . . and Dr. Salone's just on the point of concluding that deal of his. He's getting Baluze remarkably cheap—three hundred hectares under crops, and the chateau thrown in . . ."

"Never, never, never, Armand . . . not while I'm alive!"

Madame Agathe entered the room, a parcel in her

15

hands. It was the tart. A smell of almond-paste drifted through the darkness. Armand got up and took it from her. She asked where Marie was.

"In her own room, sulking because I told her father that she turned round twice."

Madame Agathe offered to go and fetch her, but Armand Dubernet was of the opinion that they had much better sit down to luncheon. It would take an age to get her into a better temper . . . and the mutton would be overdone.

"By the time Adila's finished carving . . ."

"Maybe, but don't forget there are prawns first."

2

THERE was only an attic between Marie's room and the roof. She had forgotten, before starting for church, to close the window, and the shutters were ajar. Away beyond the old and faded tiles the hillside was drowsing in a motionless blaze. She took off her muslin frock. All she wanted was to lie half naked on the bed, hugging her misery. A moment later, with her face buried in the pillow, she gave way to a wild drunkenness of tears. A bumblebee thumping against the panes, seemed as though melted into the surrounding blue. There was no one to feel pity for the childish body that was already half a woman's. The wallpaper, with its pattern of purple flowers, had been there unchanged for longer than anyone could remember. The bed was a ship's cot anchored from all eternity in the lifeless waters of this little town "from which all youth had drained." Youth had no place in Dorthe. The girl murmured a stifled name into the pillow —Gilles! Gilles! Gilles! . . . They had met only three times: once at the Mongies' picnic, twice—and those had been the real times—on the bank of the Leyrot. He had been bathing with Nicolas Plassac. He had looked like a wolf, with the drops of water glittering on his golden pelt. Nicolas was ugly and pasty. Gilles had called out that they would get dressed, and had begged her to wait for them. Nicolas had stopped a short distance away. Gilles had said—"he's going to keep 'cave' . . ." Madame Agathe had joined him. She had turned a blind eye on what was happening. They had arranged to meet again. Oh, those two hours!—she must taste their sweetness again, no matter what the cost . . . But he? . . . was he, too, suffering? He had not been to Mass for three years—had started going again only to see her. His last words had been that Madame Agathe would arrange everything. She was in love with Nicolas Plassac, he said . . . as though she were capable of being in love with anybody! For all her soft looks one never really knew what she was thinking, or why she would say one thing, and then, a moment later, something else that completely contradicted it. She could be all honey and sweetness when she liked, but really, she was an old spider, a snake in the grass, and looked as though something were eating her up. Perhaps she'd got a cancer. If only she would die! . . . Oh, no! . . . that's wicked. No, I don't want her to die! I only thought that for fun . . . Oh, please, God, keep Madame Agathe alive!

3

AT ABOUT the same time, while a young girl, half naked on her bed, was suffering agonies for his sake, Gilles was seated at table at the the house of his friend Nicolas, in the rue de la Sous-Préfecture. He was a young man of twenty-three, and remarkably like any other young man of twenty-three. There was nothing wonderful about him, except in the eyes of little Marie, and of Nicolas. Madame Plassac, Nicolas's mother, admired him, too, but then, her opinion didn't count. She regarded him as a member of local "society." It gave her no little satisfaction to think that young Salone, the son of the Doctor, who was a member of the General Council, should be a friend of her Nicolas, and be willing to take luncheon at her table; that he should approve of everything she put before him, and should actually have asked for a second helping of the grilled mutton, saying that he had never tasted better.

"Oh, Monsieur Gilles, that's just your flattering tongue. I knows as what you get at home must be a lot better, not though it mightn't be worse, for as my old man used to say, it's not always the rich as eats better than we do."

Gilles had felt at first that Nicolas might be embarrassed by this kind of talk. But Nicolas, where his mother was concerned, was blind. Just as this combination of living-and-dining-room which never got the sun, which was dark and damp, with its clock under a glass bell, and its colored lithographs in their fly-blown frames, had frequently figured in his poems as the poor but sacred home where every object throbbed with a muted life of its own, so, too, did this old woman appear to him as somehow transfigured and moving in a glow of beautiful humility.

As for Gilles, he stood in Nicolas' eyes for all the youth and loveliness, and terrible fragility of life . . . Without any sense of embarrassment, he sat gazing at this fleeting wonder of the world on which time was already laying its finger. He loved him. He did not in the least know what he was eating. He did not hear what his mother was saying, nor what Gilles was answering. It was enough for him that Gilles was there, in his home. Not one of these minutes must be lost. Blessed be God who had brought Gilles into his home, into his heart, into his life—to stay there for ever and ever. They met so seldom in Paris, saw one another in so unsatisfactory a manner . . . Nicolas slept at the Lycée where he was an usher. Gilles was busy all day long attending lectures. Besides, he belonged to others, to so many others! It was better not to see too much of him. It was well that he should live separated from what he most loved in all the world. It was Nicolas' declared belief that one can truly possess what one loves only in absence and solitude.

But during the holidays at Dorthe, his friend belonged wholly to him—though he spoke of nothing but his love for Marie—Marie was this year's bright especial star. For him it was quite enough that Nicolas should listen. Gilles never felt bored in his company, because only with Nicolas could he talk about Marie. Even now he could not keep away from the subject, but took advantage of Madame Plassac's dartings in and out of the kitchen, to speak of what was in his mind.

"She turned round twice," he said.

"No, three times."

"Are you sure?—but Galigaï turned round, too . . . Ah! I thought that would make you blush!"

"Oh, please, Gilles, don't start on Madame Agathe!"

"It's not *my* fault if Galigaï adores you, is it?"

"Why d'you call her Galigaï?" asked Madame Plassac. Nicolas hid his face in his hands.

"Listen, Gilles—the only thing that comforts me about the holidays being nearly over is the knowledge that there'll once more be hundreds of miles between her and me . . . she won't suddenly appear when I'm not expecting her . . . she . . . she . . . rapes my room!"

"You know what you promised me, that you would never break with her. She's our only hope, Marie's and mine. If she rapes your room, and you, too, into the bargain, well, that's just too bad!"

"Oh, Gilles!"

Gilles laughed, as he always did when he had succeeded in shocking his friend.

"What are you two talking about?" asked Madame Plassac.

She had a huge dish in her hands containing a mass of soggy pastry stuck full of plums—the kind that the people of Dorthe can always manage to tuck away after even the most copious of meals.

"We were talking of Madame Agathe," said Gilles.

"Oh, her!"

"Don't you like her?" asked Gilles with hypocritical innocence.

"Comes in here, she does, as though we kept open house! Never has so much as a word for me, but goes straight up to Nicolas's room, as bold as brass . . . Shouldn't wonder, I shouldn't, if she's got designs on him!"

"Oh, mother, please!" exclaimed Nicolas, with a look of horror.

"The last time, I give her a piece of my mind. Oh yes, I settled *her* hash! Don't much think I shall catch *her* on the stairs again!"

"But, Madame Plassac," said Gilles with an air of great

seriousness, "you know, don't you, that she is Monsieur de Camblanes' daughter . . . a Count's daughter!"

"I know all about that! A fine Count as sends out his girl to work for her living all along of his making free with her savings! . . . and when I says work for her living, well, we all know what sort of work she does along of Monsieur Dubernet!"

Nicolas said again—"Oh, mother, please!" and shut his eyes because he could not bear to see his mother as she was at that moment. Gilles was enjoying himself hugely. "Poor Galigaï!" he sighed, and once again Madame Plassac asked, "Who's this Galigaï?"

"I suppose you know, Madame Plassac, that she was once married to a baron?" Gilles went on.

"Who left her in the lurch on the wedding day, oh yes! Waited till he'd got his hands on the money his grandma had promised him if he got married—every penny of two million it was . . . and then sneaked off that blessed evening while she was a-changing of her clothes . . ."

"Not really!" said Gilles.

Nicolas looked at him with melancholy eyes. When he spoke there was a note of reproach in his voice.

"But Gilles, you know as much about all that as Mamma does . . ."

Madame Plassac raised her pointed nose (she was busy

cutting the pastry). Her eyes behind their spectacles were glittering.

"And he didn't go alone, neither!"

"Who with, then?" asked Gilles with a sanctimonious air.

But Nicolas continued with his former protest: "Oh, look here, Gilles, you oughtn't to make mother talk about such things!"

"It weren't with no young woman, to be sure."

Gilles would not let the subject drop: "Who was it then?"

"If you don't know, 'tisn't for me to tell you!"

He realized from Madame Plassac's tone that he had gone too far. She half opened the shutters, and remarked that a storm was getting up. The sun had disappeared. Heavens! how indigestible that pastry had been! The bell was sounding for Vespers. There was a patter of feet outside, a babble of voices. The children of the Church Guild were trooping by. In another fifteen minutes they would be solemnly chanting the psalms in Latin, not in the least worried by the fact that they did not understand one single word of what they were saying.

4

MARIE had cried herself to sleep. The church bell failed to wake her, and so, too, did Madame Agathe when she crept softly into the room. She was carrying a tray on which were arranged six bright-red prawns, some biscuits, a few sad-looking peaches, a number of plums which the wasps had been at, and a carafe of water misted over by condensation. How pitifully young the body looked over which sorrow and sleep had fought for victory! Marie was lying with her face on her arm. One leg was bent, and the knee had the smooth look of a pebble seen through running water, a pebble which no hand had ever touched. The other leg was dangling over the edge of the bed, and a shaft of sunlight caught the faint fluff of down which seemed almost to belong to some young wild creature of the woods. From that body, slightly damp with sweat, from the graceful arms curved upwards like the handles of a basket, revealing on the underside, where they joined her shoulders, two faint patches of dark gold, a smell arose that was less animal than vegetable, a smell of earth and water, of sea-tides and garden things. Madame Agathe raised her eyes and saw herself reflected in the window-pane. Her face was blotched and bony, her Sunday blouse unlaundered. The image thus presented to her did not reveal the semi-circular sweat stains under her arms, but she knew that they were there. The blouse was too loose for her and sagged in front: "I haven't any breast!" If only that were literally true! Better, far, to have nothing at all than what she had! From where she was standing she could not see Marie's twin breasts, but she knew well enough what they looked like. The same shaft of sunlight which touched the girl's leg lay across Madame Agathe's skinny arm. Though she was holding her breath, the sleeping figure stirred. "Who's that?"

Madame Agathe pointed to the tray: "I've brought you something to eat. But first, you'd better get some clothes on."

"You ought to have knocked," said Marie. "I'd have slipped into my frock before letting you come in."

"There is nothing you can 'let' me do, because there is nothing you can forbid me."

Oh dear! now she had vexed Madame Agathe, who was her one and only hope, her last chance. She flung two thin arms about her governess' neck. What had she done? Why didn't she still love her? Madame Agathe could feel the warmth of the young body pressed to her own.

"Come now, Marie!"

She pushed the girl away, but without roughness. "Get dressed and then you shall eat."

"I'm not hungry."

"At your age one is always hungry."

She helped her charge into her muslin frock, made her sit down at the table, and helped her to the food.

"You know how fond you are of prawns. These are all your father left. He *would* go on eating: it was impossible to stop him!"

Marie raised one shoulder in her characteristic shrug. What did it matter to Gilles and her if her father stuffed himself till he burst? Suppose her father and mother vanished altogether, suppose they weren't there any longer . . . She wiped her fingers and asked: "What difference is there between the Salones and us? Why are we better than them?"

Madame Agathe's lip curled upwards revealing her teeth. They were strong teeth, but irregular, and with prominent canines. She smiled.

"You must ask your mother. I confess that the difference escapes me."

"But I want to know; what is it?"

In the smoothest of tones, the governess replied: "The difference between a black ant and a red, my dear."

"I don't understand," said Marie.

"There is nothing *to* understand, child."

27

She had been born a Camblanes. The Count, her father, came of a family which had been among the most illustrious in all Gascony during the sixteenth century. For twenty-four hours she had been the wife of the Baron de Goth. That he had gone off, on the very evening of the wedding day, in the sleeper reserved for Agathe, in the company of his father's gardener, did not alter the fact that she had borne until the marriage was annulled by the Court of Rome a name which had been ennobled by Clement V., the first of the Avignon popes. In her eyes the same muddy dregs of humanity had spawned both Salones and Dubernets. She ranked them considerably lower in the social scale than quite humble folk—the Plassacs, for example—who made no pretensions. Furthermore, she believed that she had none. Her husband of a day had left her with feelings of loathing which extended to the whole of their caste. That, at least, was the reason she had given to her father when it was necessary to overcome his opposition to her plan of seeking employment with the Dubernets as a governess. It was his pride that he believed in nothing but the soil. To it he had sacrificed everything, only to see his fortune swallowed up by the Belmonte vineyards. He had failed to renew the old plants, and had sold his grapes at the wrong times. He just managed to live on his mortgaged property. One half of his daughter's monthly salary was squandered on the Turf. The Dorthe folk said: "She has lost caste just to keep her father going." But work does not necessarily involve the loss of social status. There was no reason why Agathe should be regarded as having degraded herself. How should others know that she was moving in the direction of *somebody,* that she was lowering herself deliberately, and would go on lowering herself until she had reached the level on which he whom she sought habitually moved? With her beside him, Nicolas would go far and climb high. She would worm her way into his life, and, in the long run, would become firmly established there. At the moment, he was running from her, but there is nothing that cannot be achieved, even in love—so she thought—by sheer will-power. She had never had any genuine feelings for the wretched, girlish Bertrand de Goth. She told herself that she could have kept him had she wanted to. That she was not wholly without attractions was to be found in the fact that Armand Dubernet had a certain way of looking at her . . . She had had to have a bolt fitted to her bedroom door . . . She had only to speak, to declare herself, and this Plassac youth, the son of a woman who had looked after the chairs in the Cathedral . . . To be sure, he was afraid of being left alone with her—but that was only his shyness. She knew that she stared at him too much. She was so hungry for him!

"Madame Agathe, you're not listening to me!"

She gave a start. For all she knew, the girl might have been talking for quite a while.

"Why are you against us? After all, it's through you that I got to know him."

"You must have taken leave of your senses! The Plassac boy is a friend of mine. Young Salone merely happened to be with him—there was nothing I could do about it."

"Oh, Madame Agathe, a woman as sensitive as you are *must* have seen from the first that something was beginning between Gilles and me. You *did* see it, and you encouraged our meetings. I shall never forget that . . ."

Her face had an eager look. No, this silly little chit wasn't pretending; she really did believe that her love had touched her governess' heart! Not for a moment did she suspect that Madame Agathe had arranged those meetings for no other reason than that she might have Nicolas to herself. He was no longer avoiding her—not because he had fallen in love, on that score she had no illusions, but because he was carrying out young Salone's wishes. If Nicolas had consented to take a stroll with her in the woods, it had been only because he had wanted to leave the field free for Marie and Gilles. All the same, it had made her very happy.

She went across to the window, and pushed the shutters open. The blue of the sky had become tarnished. The coming storm showed black above the roof-tops. The swallows were flying low. The dust was lifting in little eddies, and then subsiding. The plaint rising to heaven was the exasperated buzz of worried flies. Madame Agathe turned and looked at Marie. Her face was calm. It expressed nothing at all. In a severe voice, she said: "I would never had believed, Marie, that a girl of seventeen, brought up as you have been, would dare to lose her heart to a young man, and actually think of marriage . . . Your mother fully understands the situation. She does not hold it against me that I should never have imagined that between a Dubernet and a Salone . . ."

"All the same, you said just now that there was no more difference between us than between a red ant and a black . . ."

"That was because I wanted to make you laugh. I don't like seeing you tearful."

Marie climbed onto her lap and buried her face in her blouse.

"You do love me a little, don't you?—say you do."

Yes, at this moment she really did love her a little.

"Give me a good hug," said Marie.

Madame Agathe made pretense that she was dandling a baby in her arms. In accordance with an old Camblanes formula, she started to croon in a sing-song voice, "Rock-a-bye baby."

"You're stifling me, I can't breathe, get up!" Marie smoothed her frock with the tips of her fingers. There was something sly in the way she looked at Madame Agathe.

"If only you would . . . why won't you?"

"I can't go against your mother's wishes."

The girl protested that it was in Madame Agathe's power to change those wishes. The governess denied that she had any such influence. Besides, even if she had, wouldn't she be conniving at Marie's unhappiness? After all, what sort of a person was this young Salone?

"If only you knew him!"

The governess' response was dry: "You know no more about him than I do. You have no idea what he's like . . . All you know is that you want him to take you in his arms. He's just an unlicked cub. Personally," she added with sudden violence, "I find him repellent!"

Marie thought she was joking and replied with a laugh: "Well, I don't—I most certainly don't—though I admit"—she went on with an ecstatic look—"that he's not very tidy." In fact, there was nothing about Gilles that she did not dote on, down to his tousled hair, his not very clean hands, his shorts worn rather longer than they should have been, and the smell that always hung about him—a mixture of stale tobacco, Eau-de-Cologne and a body hot from running.

There was a muted rumble.

"If only it would rain!" said Marie. "Provided there's no hail."

Her governess went to the window and stretched her hand.

"Not a drop. Listen, Marie: it's just possible that I may see him this afternoon."

The girl's eyes were shining. "At Nicolas Plassac's?" she asked.

"Maybe . . . I don't know yet. You mustn't think . . . only, if there's a message, I'll let you know . . . I don't mean a message in writing, you mustn't count on that . . . in fact, you'd better not count on anything."

"Oh, you've taken such a load off my mind!"

She gave Madame Agathe another hug.

"How can that be? All I said was that perhaps I might see him. But I'm certainly not going to look for him."

"Oh!" murmured Marie in a disappointed voice. "It's wrong of you to blow hot and cold like that. Surely you must see how on edge I am . . ."

The older woman gave the girl a long look.

"I am quite serious, Marie: you *must* try to understand."

"How, understand? What is it I've got to understand?"

Madame Agathe was still staring at her as though she were attempting to convey an unspoken thought.

"I'm afraid I'm too stupid," sighed the other.

Madame Agathe drew her close and kissed her on the forehead.

"Yes," she said, "much too stupid!"—then—"What are you going to do while I am away?" she asked.

Marie said she should wait until her mother had started for Vespers, and then go to the Cathedral herself.

"I shall get there before the *Magnificat.*"

"That's a good idea; it will take your mind off things."

"But I don't want my mind to be taken off things! I've so many requests to make."

Madame Agathe's projecting canines showed beneath her lifted lip.

"Do you mean that you talk to God about young Salone?"

"Indeed I do!—d'you think that's wicked of me?"

"Of course I don't, you little silly, not wicked at all. Come and see me in my room when I get back—I may be late."

"D'you think there'll be time for me to go to Caliot's and make up for the éclair I missed? I shall be feeling hungry by then; after all, I haven't had any proper lunch."

Oh, these Dubernets! Even this love-lorn chit could think of nothing but food! The governess took the tray. Marie tried to relieve her of it, protesting that she would carry it down herself.

"No, you must let me do that. It's what I'm paid for," said Madame Agathe.

Just as she was closing the door, she added: "Pray, but use your brain as well. The most important thing in life, my dear, is to know how to use your brain, even in matters of the heart."

5

THE rain was still holding off. Madame Agathe crossed the Place and reached the rue de la Sous-Préfecture, which led from it, opposite the Cathedral. Madame Plassac's single-storied house was the last on the left, at the far end, just before the open country began. The garden formed an angle with what the people of Dorthe called the "Boulevard," or the "Rampart Walk," though it never occurred to anyone to walk there. It was doubtful whether its stone benches had ever been sat upon. Nevertheless, for Madame Agathe it represented the beating heart of the world, especially during the holidays, when Nicolas was at home. Even when he was away, there was something sacred to her about the spot, merely because he *had* lived within call of it. Her favorite refuge was on the far side of the Boulevard, where, screened by a privet hedge, she could see, above the dining room, the window of the room which *he* inhabited at holiday-time (for the rest of the year it was Madame Plassac's). During her periods of occupancy, the window was always kept closed, and the shutters ajar. But, as soon as Nicolas turned up, except during the hottest hours of the day, the casement was flung wide open to the countryside. Nicolas' room! She no longer dared to go straight upstairs to it. On the last occasion of her doing that, Madame Plassac had spoken very sharply.

She turned the corner of the little meadow, and slipped through a hole in the hedge. The grass was still flattened at the foot of the oak tree where it was her habit to sit. She spread out her mackintosh. It was impossible to see anything in Nicolas' room, except the gleam of the wardrobe mirror. The governess pulled a book from her bag, though she had never been able to read a line here, within eyeshot of the sacred house. Then, suddenly, she saw him. A moment later, Gilles Salone came and stood beside him, with his arms upon the window-bar. They leaned out above the garden. Probably they were saying—"how good the damp earth smells"—for a few large drops were splashing upon the wilted leaves of the lime. They talked without looking at one another. Occasionally they laughed. Gilles was smoking. Nicolas did not smoke. It was one of the rules of what he called his asceticism. Because of him, Agathe also had given up tobacco. She gazed with melancholy craving at this mystery into which she could not penetrate, this communion which held no place for her, nor ever could have done, even if Nicolas had loved her. Nothing is simpler, nothing less mysteri-

ous than vice. Young Bertrand de Goth sneaking away
with his partner in sin on the very evening of her marriage was a chapter only too hackneyed, obvious, and brief,
in the records of human ignominy. But this excessively
secret alliance between two young men was something
entirely different. Each knew that he could remain in-
definitely with the other without the risk of boring him.
They shared everything—their reading, their dreams,
their passions. Even though neither spoke, the understanding between them was complete. They had their
secret language, their little tricks of speech that others
knew nothing of. Oh, how exasperated Madame Agathe
felt by the existence of this mystery, and how deeply it
tormented her!

She heard the first rain-drops on the leaves, though as
yet she could not feel them. She looked at the two large
tousled heads leaning out over the garden, and almost
touching. The trunk of the oak against which she was
leaning hurt her. The earth was hard, and, close to her
ear, a tremor sounded within the dry and barren field.
She wiped her sweating face with her handkerchief. A
drop, two drops, fell upon her forehead, into her neck,
and trickled down between her shoulder-blades. The two
boys stretched out their hands to feel the rain which now
was falling fast and heavy. Agathe got up and put on her
mackintosh. The oak sheltered her. She was blinded by

a sudden flash of lightning. The rumbling behind the livid clouds was drowned by the hiss of falling water. The window was shut. She could still catch the gleam of the looking-glass. Now and again it was obscured by the shadow of one or other of the boys.

6

MADAME AGATHE'S felt hat was dripping wet. She took it off and dried her hair with her handkerchief. This wall of rain, this house fast shut upon the impenetrable intimacy of two young men, all these ranged and reared defenses, far from proving too much for the little blood-less, storm-drenched creature, served but to rouse her from her lethargy. She stiffened her back and reminded her-self of what she had to do. Ever since Nicolas had obsessed her mind she had mastered the laws which, during the holidays, regulated the ordering of his days. On Sundays, as soon as his mother had got back from Vespers, he gave up to her the hours remaining before bedtime. When it was fine he put a shawl across her shoulders with his own hands, and pinned it with an an-tique brooch. Then, not unpleasurably aware that he was giving a display of perfect filial devotion, would take her arm and walk with her around the Place. If the weather were rainy, they would sit together by the win-dow, playing at draughts. Sometimes, though less fre-quently, he would read to her, trying to make her under-

stand the beauties that he loved in literature. She would
break in upon him with ridiculous comments, until such
time as a faint sound of snoring would warn him that he
had better continue his reading to himself. Thus, Vespers
over, Gilles would yield pride of place to Nicolas's mother,
and Agathe could rest assured that she would find him at
his father's house. But first, she must go home, change
her dress and shoes, tidy her hair. She knew well that a
strict attention to personal appearance is the trustiest
weapon of the ugly. For another half hour the house
would be empty. Armand Dubernet was at his club; his
wife and daughter in the Cathedral.

Quickly she set herself to rights, and changed into a
grey tailor-made. As she passed the door of Madame Dubernet's room, she thought she heard a groan, and
stopped. Yes, it was the sort of long-drawn animal whine
that women utter in child-bed. She pushed the door open.
Julia had not even taken off her hat and boots. Her right
hand was still gloved in black. She was lying on her side
with her knees drawn up. She hastily pulled down her
skirts so as to conceal a glimpse of black, wrinkled stockings on swollen legs, and pushed out of sight, between
the bed and the wall, a towel soiled with blackish stains.

"It's ages since I last had an attack . . . but I feel better now . . . I've taken some laudanum . . . If it weren't
for this feeling of heaviness . . ."

Madame Agathe felt her wrist, smoothed her pillow,

and then said, with a note, as it were, of restrained fervor in her voice:

"This time you're going to do as I tell you. It is your turn to obey. You're going to see a doctor and have a thorough examination."

With lips tight drawn, and a look of mulish obstinacy, Julia lay there. She made no sign nor gesture of refusal. She kept her legs pressed tightly together, and laid her two small hands, one of them still gloved, upon her stomach. She was one of those countrywomen still to be found, perhaps, even in these days, who would rather suffer agonies than reveal to the sight and touch of a man —he might be a doctor, but that made no difference—the shameful plague-spot set in the female flesh, the breeding lair of pestilence.

"You have often in the past been good enough to listen to me, Madame," went on Agathe, while she busied herself with loosening and removing the sufferer's boots: "you have often confided in me, excepting only about what is nearest to my heart—your health and your life."

The eye that Madame Dubernet opened had suddenly become shrewd and observant. Was Madame Agathe really fond of her? Madame Agathe, that strong-minded creature who had no need, as she, Julie, had, to hedge herself in, to pay lip-service to all the social prejudices and taboos of Dorthe; this governess, born a Camblanes, who had a "head of her own?" Had she a heart as well, and in that heart was there a place for her? For a moment the older woman kept within her own moist grasp the other's thin and dried-up hand.

"Don't worry too much, my dear. My mother suffered from the same trouble, and the only thing she did for it was to use compresses of Lourdes water. Whatever it was she had inside her shrivelled up, and she lived to be eighty-four. Up to the end of her life she was proud to think that she had never once submitted herself to those abominable examinations which are the shame of our sex."

She heaved a sigh, and murmured:

"I am feeling better"—and added, "If you are going to Benediction, you might bring Marie back with you."

Madame Agathe inclined an acquiescent head, though she remarked that the girl had better not be given any reason for thinking that she was being watched. The important thing was not to lose her trust.

"I rely on you entirely, my dear. Anything you do or decide will, I am sure, be for the best. She looks on me as her enemy. You are the only person on whom I can depend to prevent this terrible misfortune, and if it is God's will that I be taken . . ."

"You mustn't say such things, Julia!"

". . . I like to think that nothing here will be changed, and that Marie . . ."

She could say no more and compressed her lips. Her

nose looked pinched as though in anticipation of what was to come. She seemed to be rehearsing her part when she should be called upon to play the corpse. Once again she opened her eyes and smiled at Madame Agathe. A longing for sleep was upon her, as always after one of her "bad times." The governess remained sitting by her bed until the sound of regular breathing told her she was free to go. Her shoes creaked. Very quietly she closed the door.

Madame Agathe could rely upon the mechanical routine of all these lives. Until Vespers were over, Madame Plassac would not leave the church, and Gilles would not leave Nicolas. It was too early as yet to ring at Dr. Salone's house. She entered the Cathedral by one of the side doors. One of the Canons was saying the evening prayer before the Blessed Sacrament. Scarcely had he finished than the faithful barked the responses with a sort of gluttonous haste, and the vaulted roof echoed back the subdued growl which, rather surprisingly, was produced by the thin scattering of female worshippers. Madame Agathe sat down behind a pillar without troubling to kneel or concentrate her mind in prayer, there being nobody to see her. It was an understood thing in the Dubernet household that she should be allowed to remain true to her Jansenist traditions, which were hereditary in the Camblanes family, and should be expected to take Communion only at Easter. Whether she even did that was doubtful. Well, people could say what they liked. A reputation for heresy flattered her. Her own conviction was that she had lost her faith. But had she really done so? Had she, if it came to that, ever had a faith to lose? That, however, was a matter of mere philosophic hair-splitting. The simple fact of the matter was that she was out of communion with God, and no longer spoke with Him. Her view was that she had been unfairly treated by the Heavenly Father in the matter of gifts. She was, as one of the clergy had put it—showing himself in this more far-sighted than the Dubernet family—"kicking against the pricks." What use was there in praying? All the praying in the world would not make her less repulsive-looking, nor less flat-chested. How could so dead a soul, somebody so miserably equipped in the matter of physical charms, have any inkling of the Eternal Love? Six rows of little girls were bombarding the altar at point-blank range with their "Priez pour nous." Their fire was being directed by two aged nuns, all that remained of a local Order which could no longer find recruits. Madame Agathe waited until the Cathedral should have emptied, while the great organ (it would have taken more than a hundred thousand francs to put it to rights) emitted a series of intermittent grunts, wheezing asthmatically, like an old broken-down lion in the cluttered forest of stone.

7

GILLES had been so deep in thought as he walked down the empty Boulevard, that he reached his father's door without having been in the least conscious of where he was going. The doctor was trying in vain to get his little car going with the starting-handle. When he straightened up he was purple in the face. He had scarcely any neck. "That damned self-starter's died on me again," he grumbled. "Here, let me do it," said Gilles. A peasant lad had come to fetch the doctor to his sick grandmother. He had no idea what was the matter with her.

"She's not dead, is she? Surely you can tell me that much? Fine thing to drag me twelve miles only to find an old corpse at the end of it! I bet you she *is* dead," he added, turning to Gilles: "they always are."

"Why go then? . . . one of these days you'll be picked up in a ditch . . ." his son remarked unsympathetically.

"More than likely," replied his father. "But I was forgetting, there's someone come to consult *you,* my boy; she's in the drawing room, been waiting there for the last half hour. It's you she wants to see—your turn this time."

"Who is it?"

"I'm not going to spoil the surprise," said the doctor (when he laughed his eyes almost completely vanished) "someone who's got a good deal to tell you, I shouldn't be surprised. Go on in—hurry."

Gilles crossed the little path of sodden garden at a run, jumping over the petunia bed in his haste . . . Perhaps Marie had taken the opportunity of Vespers . . . But no, that figure bending over a pile of back numbers of "Le Monde Illustré" was certainly not Marie's. Madame Agathe got up as he entered the room. They shook hands. Gilles motioned to her to remain seated while he stood, fixing her with a fine, cold eye. Madame Agathe tried to remember how she had planned to broach the subject which had brought her there. She had had plenty of time in which to make her plans during the half-hour she had spent beneath the watchful gaze of Madame Salone from the wedding group hanging over the piano. When she had died, a few months after Gilles's birth, the doctor had taken a vow that nothing should be changed in the arrangement of the house. He had long since found consolation for his loss, but the late nineteenth-century armchairs were still adorned with ridiculous scraps of crochetwork, and the windows were still screened by torn net curtains upon the borders of which the dead woman had expended so many years of patient labor.

"No doubt you can guess the object of my visit?"

He shook his head. Surely she didn't think he was going to put himself out for her? Gilles never put himself out for anybody. Still, he might have to make an exception in the case of someone on whom depended the accomplishment of what he found himself desiring with so unusual a degree of intensity. Even now she might be useful. How, in a place like Dorthe, could one ever arrange to meet the daughter of a prosperous middle-class family without the help of an accomplice?

Galigaï was expressing herself with extreme slowness, carefully choosing her words.

"I have been placed in charge of Mademoiselle Dubernet's education. Your presence here has caused her grave disquiet . . ."

On and on she went . . . Whatever happened, he mustn't antagonize her, mustn't rub her the wrong way. Above all, he mustn't let her guess the tiniest part of the repulsion with which the mere sight of her filled him. He was the type of young man who hates young women if they do not happen to be desirable. He was terrified lest he should not be able to hide his feelings. That was why he was being so careful not to say anything, and it was almost by chance that, when she said—"I appeal to your heart"—he answered: "I have no heart, Madame."

"That I don't believe!" she exclaimed.

"Not in the sense you give the word."

Madame Agathe stopped speaking, and scanned him from head to foot. Under the force of this scrutiny, he suddenly plumped down in the chair facing hers, and pulled it forward until his great knees were almost touching her grey tailored skirt.

"What is the real reason for your coming here?" he asked.

What an oaf! She pushed her chair slightly back. He, too, inspired *her* with feelings of horror. What she hated in him was the lumbering male forcefulness which an insignificant chit of a girl could release, though a superior person like herself had not the least effect upon it.

"You're the only person who can influence Madame Dubernet," said Gilles. "I suppose you know who Nicolas compares you with?"

She flushed, thrilled to think that Nicolas should have had her in mind sufficiently to compare her with anybody.

"Léonora Galigaï . . . d'you know whom I mean?"

"Yes, indeed!" she said with a laugh. "It was Léonora Galigaï who dominated Marie de Médicis. When she was accused of magical practices, she replied that the only magic she had used was what a strong mind can exercise over a weak one. Isn't that so? But you are quite wrong if you think that Madame Dubernet is weak."

"You, at least, are strong."

"Perhaps . . ."

She sighed; then, after a brief pause:

"In the case of Nicolas Plassac appearances are deceptive. He is not weak, either."

"But he happens to be very fond of me," said Gilles.

He got up to open the window which the servant must have shut during the storm. In a low voice, as though speaking to himself, he muttered, "Oh, these anaemic-looking women, no matter how careful they are to wash . . ." He drank in the scent of wet petunias. Galigaï, he thought, was pondering some weighty reply. But in this he was wrong. She was trying to digest that "he happens to be very fond of me." This young Salone, and nobody else, could work on Nicolas. Should Nicolas Plassac ever resign himself to the idea of marrying Agathe de Camblanes, it would be simply and solely to ensure the happiness of this young barbarian with the look of an ill-tempered dog which might at any moment decide to snap. With a great effort she forced herself to speak.

"Our positions are quite different. You are under no necessity to persuade Marie . . . all you have to overcome are external difficulties . . . whereas I . . ."

"Naturally, I can't promise that I shall be successful . . ." he muttered.

He was conscious that his cheeks were flaming, and turned back to the window. Did this horrible creature really think that he was going to make her a present of Nicolas, give him to her bound hand and foot? But, after all, it was necessary for Nicolas only to pull the wool over

her eyes until he, Gilles, was safely engaged to Marie—not
a moment longer. Certainly, he would not dream of sac-
rificing Nicolas. The scent of rain-drenched petunias
would be for ever linked in his mind with the memory
of this moment when, planning basely to make use of
his friend, he had realized suddenly that he loved Nicolas more than anybody in the world, that, in all prob-
ability, he was the only person he ever *had* loved. He had
ceased to be conscious of the woman in the corner. She
might have been a bat clinging to the curtain. It was some
considerable while before he turned his head. When he
did so he stared at her before putting his next question.

"When am I going to see her? Marie, I mean . . .
when am I going to see Marie?"

"You must be mad! There can be no question of your
seeing her . . . not yet, that is. What a child you are!"

She was laughing at him.

Everything that she had come to say had been said. She
got up and held her hand out to Gilles. He merely touched
it with the tips of his fingers.

"You must think me a very stupid woman!"

He flushed and looked away. She had seen through
him, all right. There was nothing more to be said. Not a
word need be added.

8

THE Dubernets were sitting at dinner in the garden, without a lamp. The moon was shining through the branches of the giant tulip-tree. Monsieur Dubernet was dawdling over his cheese. Marie, as though poised above her chair on invisible wings, was trembling with nervous impatience. She had had almost no talk with Madame Agathe, because her mother, perhaps suddenly suspicious, had followed her into the governess' room almost at once.

Armand Dubernet suddenly startled them with an unexpected question. They had assumed that he was digesting his food, whereas, actually, he had been deep in thought.

"Agathe, did you read those new Montesquieu fragments in *La Revue?*"

"It's getting quite chilly," Julia Dubernet remarked sharply.

Fifteen years earlier, before Armand had become sluggish and spiritless, this sort of remark would have been characterized by him as "one of Julia's charges of buckshot" by means of which, and with unerring accuracy, she would bring down the bird of conversation in full flight. As it was, he broke off all attempt at discussion, and returned to his Roquefort. Marie got up, eager for departure, but her mother called her back.

"Stay where you are, until I give the signal!"

Marie settled down once again on her perch. Armand Dubernet emptied his glass and wiped his moustache.

"No need to wait for me, m'dear, no need at all." He took a cigar from his waistcoat pocket, and rolled it in his fingers to make it crackle. Marie had already vanished. She had said to Madame Agathe, "I shall be on the terrace." But the governess was in no hurry to join her. Julia was watching. She may have thought there was something in the wind . . . But, no, that couldn't be, because what she said to Agathe was:

"I'm going to lie down. The pain's gone, but I feel exhausted. Don't leave Marie alone. For all we know that boy may be snuffling about below the terrace, on the river bank. Young men of that age are just like a lot of dogs."

Agathe stayed for a moment or two with Armand.

"You must be sensible," she said to him. "I have got to keep an eye on the girl."

He made no attempt to keep her from going, but sat there grumbling, because he had let his cigar go out.

"Here I am," said Marie from the darkness.

Madame Agathe leaned beside her on the balustrade. The moon was getting up. The Leyrot was invisible, but its cool breath rose from the meadow grasses and the line of alders.

"Don't keep me waiting," Marie begged. "Tell me what happened."

She snuggled up against her governess as though the latter had been Gilles himself. Less than an hour ago Madame Agathe had seen and spoken with him.

"What a little pussy-cat you are!"

The older woman was smiling. She felt relaxed, and as though vaguely touched by some softening influence—not of happiness, nor even of approaching happiness. The mere possibility of happiness was enough to loosen her tenseness. Poor Galigaï! She might frighten the people of Dorthe, but how complete would be her surrender, how freely the tears of love would flow, when there should be a man's shoulder for her to lean against, a man's arms to hold her tight!

"There's nothing to tell," she said. "He is thinking about you all the time, and feels by no means discouraged. What more can I say than that?"

Hastily she drew away from the girl.

"Here's your mother!"

Julia had said that she was going to lie down. What if she had been trying to lay a trap? What had she guessed?

"I've brought you out a coat," she said to Marie. "That shawl isn't warm enough. Give it to Madame Agathe."

Madame Dubernet leaned her arms upon the balustrade. She was between Marie and her governess. Was it suspicion or jealousy that had brought her down? Her words gave nothing away.

"There is no ring round the moon," she remarked, "more's the pity. A little more rain wouldn't have done any harm. Look how hard the ground is . . . these showers don't penetrate . . . You haven't forgotten, Marie, have you, that you've got to take the Dutrieux boy through his Catechism? His parents don't want to have to put off his First Communion. Personally, I think the clergy are a little too exacting. What can one expect of these children of drunks?—so long as he knows what the Real Presence means . . . What's that? Oh, I thought you said something."

Marie had not uttered a word. Her mother seemed quite determined not to move. Better go straight up to bed. Madame Agathe would come and give her a good-night kiss.

Nicolas and Gilles had agreed to meet on the Castillon road, just outside the town. Nicolas was walking with his face turned skywards. He was a creature of the darkness. The summer night revealed to him the one aspect of the world with which he was familiar. Now, however, it was not to the rustle of leaves, to the distant barking of dogs, or the crowing of cocks deceived by the mock daylight of the moon, that he was listening, but to the sound

made by Gilles's boots on the hard surface of the road, to
the measured rhythm of his friend's stride keeping pace
with his own. Their twin and long-drawn shadows, now
and again intermingled, seemed to move in obedience to
some mysterious law. It was as though the two boys
formed, between them, one of the constellations of the
night sky. Gilles was talking: on and on he talked, and his
words were, for Nicolas, the measure of that living silence
of the night which is the very peace of God. He had only
too sure a presentiment of what Gilles would ask of him,
and wanted to postpone for as long as possible the moment when he would have to say "No."

"The reason you can't believe I love her is that you've
made up your mind once and for all that I am incapable
of love. You won't believe me, and you can't possibly
know. You see, you've never felt the need of love. Poetry
satisfies you completely, poetry and friendship . . . what
it comes to is that *I* satisfy you, that you don't feel the
need of anything or anyone but *me* . . . isn't that so?"

He did not wait for Nicolas to answer, but went on.

"It's perfectly natural that you shouldn't want me to
get married. I don't blame you for that. Marriage would
mean that things would never again be quite the same
between us."

All that Nicolas said was, "Oh Gilles!" They reached
the spot where the road crossed the Leyrot, and leaned on
the parapet of the bridge, as they always did, because they

loved the smell of the running stream. Gilles took out a cigarette and snapped his lighter. The flame revealed for a moment the lines so strangely etched on the forehead, and at the corners of the mouth, of the young face, the smudge of incipient beard upon the cheeks. Then it went out, and all that was visible in the radiance of the moon was a vague blur half hidden in the shadows.

He said:

"You must forgive me. I'm not really a very nice character, and suffering makes me worse . . ."

They had sat down on the parapet. They could hear the water rippling over the pebbles at the spot where, as children, they had taken off their shoes and stockings to paddle.

Nicolas laid his hand on his friend's head.

"You're so young"—he sighed.

"Marie—Marie Dubernet . . ." said Gilles. "It all seems very extraordinary to you, doesn't it—come on, admit that it does."

Nicolas said nothing, and he continued: "I must say, it seems pretty incredible to me, too. Perhaps it means that I have been saved!"

"But you've no more need than anybody else to be saved: why, more than anybody else?"

"Oh, come!" said Gilles in a low voice. ". . . don't talk as though you didn't know everything about me, even to the things I've never confessed . . ."

"You're no different from other boys of your age."

"Do you really think so?" said Gilles: then, after a long-ish silence: "It would only mean playing her up for a short while, only until the Dubernets had got used to the idea . . ."

Nicolas made one last effort to pretend he did not understand to whom his friend was referring. Gilles grew impatient.

"Why, Galigaï, of course!" he exclaimed. "She won't be easy to convince, I know that. She'll probably insist on some sort of a promise, perhaps a definite engagement which you'd have to pretend to agree to, and to keep secret at all costs . . ."

Nicholas could not keep from voicing a protest.

"No! . . . how can you suggest such a thing! I wouldn't do it for the world. I've caused her enough unhappiness, as it is . . ."

The other moved a little further off. Nicolas could feel that his mood had changed.

"Gilles," he said, "do please try to understand. It is I, not you, who am bad. I am moved to pity for others, except only for the woman who loves me. The passion I have inspired in this poor creature, and do not share, alone leaves me unmoved. It actually irritates me so much, that it drives me into a perfect frenzy . . . and now, you're suggesting . . ."

"Don't be a fool!" exclaimed Gilles. "Can't you see that

57

you would be giving her at least a few weeks of happiness? Thanks to you, she'd have had that. What is the difference, after all, between happiness and the illusion of happiness?"

"You really think me capable . . ."

Nicolas felt deeply shocked, almost outraged. He could scarcely speak intelligibly. Gilles walked away from the parapet, then came back to it. A hard note had crept into his voice.

"Don't worry. I never really believed you *were* capable of it. Shall I tell you what you are? You're just about the most repellent sort of character imaginable—a prig, with all your damned ledgers neatly balanced for the Judgment Day! If I've fallen out of love with virtue, it's because of you!"

Nicolas raised both his hands: "I virtuous?—you must be mad."

He laughed; he forced himself to laugh.

"Of course you are. You don't really care about anything except a theory of perfection which you've carefully thought out. Aren't I right?"

"And what about you?" said Nicolas. "You're not precisely *trying* to be a swine, I imagine?"

"Me? I've done things for my friends which I wouldn't admit, not even to you. A friend is someone who'd help you throw a corpse into the river without so much as asking a question!"

"Well, don't rely on me to provide the corpse."

There was an edge to Nicolas' voice. Gilles uttered a short exclamation and started to walk away in the direction of Dorthe. Nicolas, still seated on the parapet, listened to the sound of his footsteps dying away in the distance. They filled his universe. He got up and broke into a run. By the time he overtook Gilles he was out of breath. His friend did not once turn to look at him.

"Look here," panted Nicolas, "I've got an idea . . . I think I can arrange matters, but you've got to give me a little time to think it over . . ."

Gilles breathed more freely. He was touched to think that Nicolas should show himself so weak where he was concerned, but he gave no sign of what he was feeling.

"It's already September" was what he said: "we mustn't let things hang on for too long. We might find the ground cut from under our feet. She's a very strong-minded woman—you do realize that, don't you?"

They walked on for a while in silence, each occupied with his own secret thoughts. Suddenly Gilles put a question: "D'you think you really *could* bring yourself to . . . I mean, with Galigaï?"

Nicolas broke in: "Stop it! . . . that's a filthy thing to say!"

"I suppose *I* just *might*," went on Gilles broodingly: "but it would have to be . . ."

He laughed. Horrible things poured from his lips. The

night was the night no longer. Gilles had profaned it. The Cathedral looked like some enormous Ark left stranded by an ebbing flood—something given over to the predatory rats of a rotting countryside. They had reached Madame Plassac's door.

"No, don't come up," said Nicolas.

9

HE DID not strike a light in the stair well. Perhaps his mother was asleep. But no, he heard the thin, high-pitched summons "Nicolas." When he was at home, she slept in a tiny room on the ground floor. He entered without knocking, and stood beside her bed, close to the pillow. She had taken out her false teeth, and her lips and cheeks were sunken. Her eyes, without their spectacles, looked hard, bright, inhuman. They might have been the eyes of a fish or a bird.

"You stay out too late: I couldn't lock up. It'll be your fault if I'm murdered."

He heaved a sigh; why wouldn't she let him have a key?

"A fine thing that—and have you lose it!"

Once, twelve years before, he had, in fact, lost one, and Madame Plassac had never stopped talking of the event. The lock had had to be changed. She had kept the lock-smith's bill. Nicolas spoke irritably:

"What do you want me to do, then—climb in through the window?"

"Do? Stay at home of an evening with your mother, who's worked herself to the bone for you, and refused to marry again—not that I didn't have plenty of chances—and went out a-charring to pay your school bills, and did laundering for the rich folk, until the Canon gave me that there job in the Cathedral, knowing as how the chair money would be in good hands . . ."

"Have I shown myself to be an ungrateful son?" asked Nicolas in a flat voice.

"You're a good son—in words. I'm not denying that. All the same, you like to run wild with that young no-good at nights."

"That's not fair, mamma! . . . you've always said he was so nice . . ."

"It was so's not to upset you . . . I can read you like a book, I can!" A flicker of malice showed in her eyes. Nicolas remembered a poem he had once written: "Poor woman with the furrowed brow; my mother, she, who loves me well." She was well away: "They all agree in Dorthe as young Salone's a no-good. What you see in him beats me."

He bent low over the terrible face, and touched it lovingly with his lips.

"You must go to sleep," he said.

But she was still in a grumbling mood: "You might at least answer me when I ask a question. I'm not an old looney, not yet."

He made a valiant effort to summon up a smile, turned at the door, and blew her a kiss.

He climbed the stairs slowly, as though he were carrying a burden, as though a heavy beam were cutting into his shoulder. He lit the oil lamp. He had lost, this evening, his power of self-deception. He had seen his mother as she really was, and so, too, he was seeing his room.

There was a damp stain, which grew daily larger, on the soot-grimed ceiling. The wallpaper was speckled with crushed flies. From the mahogany bedside commode —which he never used—came a smell which proved, beyond a doubt, that it was put to nightly use when Madame Plassac renewed her tenancy. The Indian shawl, which he had always pretended to think valuable, and used as a tablecloth, that selfsame shawl which he had so often glorified in verse, was full of moth holes, and smirched here and there with the indelible marks of candle-grease. There was a greasy patch on the back of the wing chair, just where Gilles was accustomed to rest his head. Gilles! Gilles!—already through the thinning mists of youth a few telltale features of the man he would become within the next ten years were showing.

Nicolas blew out the lamp. The smell of hot oil gradually dispersed. His eyes grew accustomed to the half-darkness. The moon had vanished now, leaving behind her a milky pathway in the sky. A few clouds showed vaguely, like the uncertain shores of a lake of nothingness in which there twinkled a single star. Nicolas Plassac looked at it. He was putting off for as long as possible the moment when he would have to face the thought which had come to him as he ran to overtake Gilles on the road to Dorthe. "I've got an idea . . . but you've got to give me a little time . . ." An idea . . . what an idea! The sheer horror of it held him fascinated. He would be obedient to Gilles's behest—but not to the point of lying. The promise he would give to Galigaï should be no false promise.

He need not yet peer into the abyss, and measure with his eyes its terrible depths. For months, perhaps for years, he would be separated from it by his mother, who hated Agathe, and whose opposition he would have to overcome; by poverty, too, by that especially, for how could he support a home, seeing that he could scarcely buy food enough to satisfy his hunger?

But their engagement should be a genuine engagement. Nearly four hundred miles would lie between them, and all that he need have of Galigaï would be her letters. She wrote good letters. He, too, would write to her, as often as she wanted him to. That was all very well, but, sooner or later, the inevitable would have to be faced . . . Deliberately he pictured the moment . . . separate beds? . . . separate rooms? . . . nothing, he thought, would

suffice short of a dividing wall, a wall with a locked door.
Even so, it would need time for him to get used to the
idea . . . His imagination leapt the gap which separated
him from his child—for there would be a child. That
would compensate him for everything. Madame Agathe's
child . . . well, what of it? Her features were not too bad,
all that she needed to be almost pretty was a little happiness. How she had blossomed out that day when he had
taken her walking in the woods so that Gilles might have
a little while alone with his Marie . . . She had become
quite a different creature . . . yes, but too tightly strung.
Impossible to talk calmly with her. Without a word of
warning her breath had started to come short and quick,
her eyelids to flutter, her throat to swell. He tried hard to
come to terms with a certain picture in his mind's eye, a
picture of the kind he usually did his best to turn from—
the first time, in that house in the Meriadek quarter of
Bordeaux . . . the woman had said: "now don't get all
worked up." In the long run everything had been perfectly all right. Gilles would be saved, Gilles would be
happy. No, that wasn't true; he wouldn't be happy, but
at least he would find peace, repose. He would grow into
the sort of man Nicolas had seen so often at High Mass,
with a roll of fat at the back of his neck, because he was
wearing a stiff collar. Gilles! Nicolas let his mind wander
back to the early days of their friendship. He thought of

the long walks they had taken together through Paris, of the night when they had collapsed, dog-tired, onto a bench in front of the Madeleine, of the poem he had recited in a low voice. Gilles had said: "How lovely it would be if we could die together here, before the dawn."

I OUGHT to have gone with Marie," said Madame Dubernet. "I don't like to think of her being alone at the Mongies."

Armand voiced a protest.

"You know the doctor said you must rest . . ."

He was leaning on his elbows at the window. It was half open, though four o'clock had not yet sounded. But, since the day of the great storm, the heat had been diminishing. He lit a cigarette, but scarcely had he done so than she started to complain: "Oh, *please,* not in my room."

He pitched it into the garden. Agathe took the empty cup which Madame Dubernet held out to her.

"I'll go and fetch her soon, and bring her back."

"It's almost a certainty that the Salone boy will have been invited. The Mongies don't seem to mind whom they have these days."

"She promised me that she would avoid him," said Madame Agathe: "that she wouldn't exchange a single word with him."

"But they will look at each other, and looks can say

such a lot . . . She makes me feel thoroughly ashamed. When I think that she is my daughter . . ."

"I must say . . ."

Armand left the sentence unfinished, and went back to the window. There was a brief silence; then, Madame Dubernet began to complain once more: "Really, I don't know why I pay the slightest attention to that third-rate country doctor. Whenever I go to see him he has to look up all the answers in a book. He strikes me as being a perfect ninny . . ."

"But since you complain of that feeling of heaviness when you walk . . . though I do admit," went on Monsieur Dubernet, "that a young fellow like that can't possibly have had as much experience as Dr. Salone."

His wife raised a drawn and haggard face from her cushions.

"You're surely not suggesting that I should consult *that* shifty creature . . ."

"You know," said Monsieur Dubernet, "that he's no keener on this marriage than you are!"

"What nonsense! Where did you hear that story?"

He was about to reply, "Why, from Madame Agathe . . ." but the governess was staring meaningly at him, with her finger to her lips. He said: "It's the talk of the place. I gather that since he bought Baluze, our good doctor has been planning ahead . . . Names have been mentioned . . . we'd be surprised, they tell me, if we knew

. . . Big Business in Bordeaux is beginning to cast sheeps' eyes at the landed properties out this way."

"Much good may it do them." Julia Dubernet showed signs of being seriously put out, but she went on: "Folk from Bordeaux will put up with what we wouldn't touch with a barge pole. Anyhow, after they've made a few enquiries . . . What the people of Dorthe may be saying leaves me entirely cold," she finished up angrily.

"What can you expect?" interposed Agathe. "That sort of person doesn't understand that there are those to whom money is not everything . . . They and you belong to two different species. I might tell them till I was blue in the face that Marie will have money enough for two. You know the idiotic way they have of saying—'those with some want more'—it's just about as far as their minds go."

"There's something in it, all the same," said Armand Dubernet under his breath. "By the bye," he went on, "I am given to understand that the fools who sold Baluze threw in the library. According to the Sous-Préfet, there's some pretty valuable stuff in it."

"Yes, I know," said Madame Agathe. "Word's gone round up at the College that it contains a first edition of one of the *Provinciales*—with marginal comment by the great Arnould himself."

"I don't see how that can be, since . . ."

Madame Dubernet cut him short: "D'you know,

Agathe, I think it might be as well if you didn't wait till
five, but went along to the Mongies at once."

"I'll accompany you as far as the club," said Armand.

"No, please stay here. I have no wish to be left alone.
They don't hear me downstairs when I ring the bell. Besides, you'd only sit there drinking . . ."

With the air of one bestowing a great favor she added:
"You can smoke if you want to; after all, with the window open . . ."

He lowered himself heavily onto a footstool, and took
a packet of Caporals from his pocket.

Madame Agathe saw at the first glance that Marie had
been as good as her word. She was standing at some distance from Gilles, in a group of guests watching a game
of tennis. She was quite the most distinguished girl there
—so fine-drawn, and yet, at the same time, with a look of
sensuality—a sort of earthy fragility, thought Madame
Agathe. Among all the other plump little fillies, all bot-
toms and "buns" and pink and blue hair-ribbons, Marie
showed as tall and slender, with her narrow hips, and the
small, high breasts which, somehow, made one forget
everything else about her. He, meanwhile, was at the far
end of the garden, standing by the refreshments, with
arms crossed and a scowl on his face, because he was feeling ill at ease. His hair, in spite of all the brilliantine he
had lavished on it, was standing up like a cock's comb.

His face looked red because of the starched collar he was wearing. He, too, seemed to bear no resemblance to the other young men, several of whom were already putting on weight. They all had the same necks, the same hands. She understood now why Nicolas had said one day that there was something "angelic" about Gilles—"darkly angelic" were the words he had used. The Salone boy no longer irritated her. She had ceased to be jealous. She exchanged a few words with Madame Mongie and the ladies who were gathered round her. Nobody asked her to sit down. She might be her father's daughter, but she was here among them only as a governess. As she moved away, somebody said:

"I don't know what's coming over Madame Agathe, she's looking quite coquettish!"

"I know what it is, she's taken to washing her neck."

"I rather think there's something in the wind . . ."

There was a general burst of laughter. Madame Agathe threaded her way through the various groups. Making a short détour she approached the refreshments. Gilles came up to her and said, "How d'you do." She made a brief reply, and, after a few words, turned her back on him. But she had had time to whisper: "I shall be on the Castillon road at nine this evening. Tell Nicolas. Marie will be waiting for you on the terrace." Had he understood? She could not stay with him a moment longer for fear of arousing suspicion. She had probably hung about too long already. She went up to Marie and said, "Come." The girl begged for "just a moment or two more." Madame Agathe said in a low voice:

"You'll be seeing him this evening."

"Ah!" sighed the girl. Her face had gone quite white. She clung to her governess' arm. Madame Agathe murmured, "Little silly! little idiot! little fool!"

"I adore you!" said Marie.

"Don't look at him, we'll slip away."

"The old cat's dragging her off," said Madame Mongie.

1 1

STRANGE how much light the waning moon could give. Madame Agathe, so as not to be seen, was picking her way between the piles of flint and the ditch. She was feeling anxious, so certain had she felt that Nicolas would be waiting for her on the outskirts of the town. Perhaps Gilles had not understood her message, or had passed it on in a garbled form. She decided to go as far as the point where the road crossed the Leyrot. She could already catch the marshy smell, could already hear the croaking of the frogs. Almost directly over her head an owl hooted. Suddenly, she saw him. He was sitting on the parapet, in the shadows. He got up. She went straight to him. He said:

"Sit down, you can't be seen from the road."

She waited, but he did not kiss her. The idea never so much as crossed his mind.

"Are they together?" he asked. "D'you think they're running any risk?"

"What risk?" she said, drily. "Madame Dubernet is ill. Besides, if somebody did catch them, it might be the sim-

plest solution . . . it would at least force her parents'
hands."

Nicolas still said nothing. He might have been one of
the stones of the bridge. He might have been the great
pine standing there with its roots in the water of the
stream. She added: "Of course, I should lose my place.
But I shall have to leave them sooner or later, if I am to go
with you."

He came suddenly awake.

"No, Agathe, no . . . you're surely not thinking of
doing any such thing? You mustn't lose your place! Nothing's settled; I haven't said a word to my mother yet."

"What are you waiting for?" she asked. He stammered
something about having taken the first steps. He must, he
said, go carefully.

She broke in on him: "You can leave your mother to
me. I have ways and means of overcoming *her* objections.
It won't take long."

How sure she was of herself! How straight to the point
she went! He felt nervous. He had counted on its taking
a long time to win his mother over. They might even
have to wait until she was dead. That was what he had
hoped. His mind was at peace because his mother would
so certainly say "no"—would dig her toes in. And now,
here was this obstinate, strong-minded creature proposing to change all that! He said: "You don't know my
mother!"

"But you know me . . ." she replied: "and when I have set my heart on something . . ."

He put a question with an air of feigned indifference: "What are you going to say to her?"

"That's my secret," she said. "In a week from now your mother will be urging you to fix the day. You see if she doesn't."

He shuddered. She was just boasting—or, perhaps, trying to trap him.

There was a short silence. He broke it at last.

"Fix the day? How can I do that? I've got to wait till I've saved enough money to set us up in a home of our own."

He had said "us"—that was something gained!

"But I shall be working, too; I shan't cost you a penny. I've never cost anyone a penny. I'm already looking about for a job in Paris, and I've had one or two offers. Besides," she added on a note of passion, "one room's all we shall need. A single meal a day, at a bistro, will be enough for us. I've been well trained. I'm used to cooking noodles over a spirit-lamp. I lived once for a whole winter on heated-up noodles."

Such talk bruised the secret roots of Nicolas' being, struck straight at his worship of the simple sanctities of human life. He had a passion for poverty, but it must be poverty decked and beautified. He liked to think of himself as the center of an ordered domestic interior, where everything should be bathed in a timeless radiance. He attached a religious significance to the delicious smell of the family soup, to fruit set out on china plates, to long and silent meals. All this talk of spirit-lamps and reheated noodles! It hadn't taken Galigaï long to hit on the one thing which would most surely fill him with disgust!

She said nothing. She was intimidated by the fierce silence which he had raised like a wall between them. Fumblingly, she stretched a hand. He did not withdraw his own. She clasped it. Hers was like some noisome little animal, with death in its fangs. He could feel her pressing against him. He did not move away. She leaned her head against his shoulder. She had taken off her beret. He sat there as motionless as a tree-trunk. She said, "I want to feel the beating of your heart!" Would she dare? Yes, she was going to dare, all right! She slipped her fingers beneath his shirt. He suddenly felt the little claw on his bare skin. She said, "I can't feel it beating." How could that petrified heart of his have beaten? Her breath was coming fast. He knew what she would say next.

"Give me a kiss; you've never kissed me yet."

She offered her lips.

"No," he said: "your eyes . . . It is your eyes that I love."

What he meant was: it is only your eyes I could bear to touch with my lips without feeling sick.

Yet, the words he had flung at her made her thrill with happiness.

At this same moment, beneath the Dubernets' terrace, there was a sound of sighs so softly breathed, that the lopsided and eroded moon, late-rising, thought them but the rustling of leaves, and took no notice. "No," said Marie, "you'll tear my blouse . . . there, now, that's better." She said again: "Oh, I can't breathe!" Never had she imagined that a kiss could last so long. She recovered enough breath to say: "We'd be much more comfortable lying down."

"No!" he protested: "no! no!"

Such was the miracle that kept the moon suspended motionless above the great tulip-tree. She, the child, was all surrender, while he, the male-wolf had checked himself this side of innocence, nor sought to know more of her body's mystery than the fruit of parted lips, than the throbbing throat which he could completely circle with his large, ungainly hand.

"Are you both mad? D'you know what time it is?"

The moon had disappeared. Galigaï's vague bulk was visible against the terrace wall. Their mouths drew apart, but they made no movement.

"Tomorrow, darling!" he said passionately. "We *must*

meet tomorrow—I don't care where, but we *must* meet! I can't let a day go by now without holding you in my arms!"

"Yes, tomorrow," she said, and again, "tomorrow!"

Tomorrow, and every day of their lives. He vanished into the willows that fringed the tow-path. She gained the terrace by a steep track.

"I only hope mamma's asleep!"

"You're quite safe. She's taken a dose of veronal."

Marie entered the governess' room where the lamp had been left burning. Agathe looked at her. She noticed the disordered blouse, the puffy lips, the dreamy, far-away look beneath the tousled hair. Perhaps to forestall a possible reprimand, or because she felt the need to be kissed and petted, the girl flung her arms about the other's neck, but almost at once loosed them again.

"You're crying, Madame Agathe! why are you crying? You saw him, didn't you? Are you crying because you're happy?"

Her governess made no answer. It was not that she was jealous. The tide of her desire had ebbed, leaving behind it a sense of bitter tenderness without trace of hope. She did not wipe away her tears. She did not care who saw them.

12

WHEN a fragment of the moon showed next evening between the branches of the great tulip-tree, no human sighs were mingled with the rustling of the leaves. Thither, where the grass still showed trodden, Marie and Gilles had not returned. Something had happened. Madame Agathe, in Nicolas' room, was telling the two friends about it. At dawn that day Julia Dubernet had been seized by so violent an attack of pain that it had been necessary to send for the young doctor. He had been at his wits' end and had called in his colleague, Salone. No one had thought to ask the sick woman's permission. The older man had had her taken straight into Bordeaux. They had already waited too long, he said. Marie, too, had left the house with her father.

"Armand begged and implored, but all to no purpose. Julia insisted on my staying here for two days to keep an eye on things. From the instructions she gave me, it is clear that she thinks it unlikely that she will ever come back. Perhaps she has a feeling that her end is near. Nobody could face death more calmly."

She sat as though enthroned in Gilles's special chair—
("in *my* chair, the slut!")—just as though she were in
her own house, as though she had been made free of
Nicolas, and of all Nicolas' private world. And Nicolas
did not seem in any way put out!

"Do you think all is well with her—spiritually, I
mean?"

"With Julia Dubernet? Oh, you can be easy on that
score! She is convinced that all is as it should be between
her and God. She has arranged everything, down to the
last detail—not excluding a few highly meritorious acts
of charity about which nobody knows—except He and
she. She is not worrying about God. But if she discovered
that He didn't exist after all, she wouldn't show the slightest surprise. There's nobody more matter-of-fact than
these old Catholic dames."

"Yet, Julia Dubernet has an immortal soul," murmured Nicolas: "a strange idea when one comes to think
of it."

"My father," said Gilles, "told me that if what's wrong
with her is what he thinks, she must be pretty far gone.
All the same, she may drag on for quite a while. Still,
whatever happens," he added without making any attempt to hide his joy, "we're in luck's way. Everything's
bound to go swimmingly now."

Galigaï interpreted the words as meaning—we don't
need *you* any longer.

"Oh yes," she said, and there was a sharp edge to her voice, "you certainly are, as you put it, in luck's way, because you'll have only me to deal with now."

Gilles was almost speechless. "What right have you . . ." he spluttered. She got up and took her bag from the table.

"That is something you will find out soon enough—to your cost."

Nicolas stayed her with a gesture.

"I don't understand what you mean," he said: "everything is settled, isn't it?"

Galigaï gave him a long, straight stare. He did not quail. "No matter what happens?" she asked. He bowed his head in assent. She drew him to her and folded him in a clumsy embrace. Gilles had moved across to the window. She took a handkerchief from her bag and wiped her eyes.

"Dear Nicolas, I never really doubted you. Your mother's expecting me," she added. "I promised I'd go and see her as soon as I could. She is longing to hear all about the Dubernets . . . But it's about *us* that I want to talk to her."

"No, no—not yet!"

The cry had been forced from him. But she was adamant. What point was there in waiting? Time was short. She had to join the Dubernets in Bordeaux; she had given Armand her solemn word to do that. She would be at the nursing home night and day. He couldn't manage without her.

"What are you going to say to my mother?" Nicolas looked away.

"I want that to be a little surprise for you. You'll hear all about it from her this evening . . . you see if you don't!"

She wrinkled her nose. Her lip lifted in a smile, revealing her prominent teeth.

"You're not going to tell her we're engaged?"

There, it was out now.

She gave him a roguish look.

"Ah, that's my little secret!"

She was determined, she was triumphant. She knew precisely what she was going to do.

"And now, I'm going downstairs to see your mother. Till this evening—nine o'clock on the Castillon road."

No sooner had she left the room than Gilles could contain himself no longer: "The bitch!" he said. "The slut!"

Nicolas laid a hand over his mouth.

"You've got her all wrong," he said, and then, in a lower voice: "I shall have a lifetime in which to find out what she's really like . . ."

"You're afraid of her; she terrifies you, it's no good your saying she doesn't."

He had no intention of saying anything of the sort.

Still, when he had given his word, it had not been out of fear. He let his gaze rest on Gilles who averted his own and went back to lean his elbows on the window sill. The swallows were preparing to migrate early this year. They were gathering already, screaming and squabbling in the lime tree over some invisible prize. *His* prize was Marie, and he hadn't got her yet. Galigaï was still a danger. It had been no empty threat that she had uttered. What a fool he had been to defy her! Better not take any risks. Let the poor, silly fly get caught in the web, there'd always be time to save him at the last moment. He turned back into the room and slumped down in the chair. Nicolas had opened a book but was not reading it. He could hear through the floor the sound of a laugh, Galigaï's laugh, interrupted by what sounded like a man's voice. His mother's tones had grown deeper with advancing age.

He was not looking at the swirl of chattering swallows, but at a cloud of tiny flies caught in a sunbeam. Weren't they all of them, Dubernets and Camblanes, Plassacs, Salones, and Mongies, just so many agitated specks? From impenetrable depths within himself he could feel a sense of anguish welling up which, had he been alone, would have sent him to his knees. But there, outlined in the window-frame, stood the ephemeral creature who hid God from him. "Gilles!" he called. The other turned: his face was hard and set.

83

"Throw me a cigarette. I'm going to start smoking again, and be hanged to it!"

"I'll leave the packet with you," said Gilles.

It was the first time they had ever parted without having arranged to meet again.

Nicolas dared not go down. He was afraid that he might run into Galigaï and his mother. He could hear their voices still, in thrust and counter-thrust, through the floor, could make out clearly Madame Plassac's acquiescent, almost servile, inflections, and Galigaï's, the laugh she never used in private talk, her "official," "visitor's" laugh. What a long time she was staying!—into what a state of agreement the two adversaries seemed suddenly to have come! Who was he?—that he might not know the answer to that question, that he might remain forever in ignorance of it, he had schooled himself to live in a deep dream, and had given it an ever increasing solidity. He had dug a hole for himself, but had gone to ground in vain. He could hear the sounds of the probing pick coming closer and closer.

There was a knock at the door. He gave a start.

"I'm not coming in," called Galigaï. "I only just wanted to say . . ."

"But do come in . . ."

He had thrown the door open, but she shook her head.

"No, really I won't . . . I only wanted to tell you not

to wait for me on the Castillon road this evening. I shall come here instead. It will be much more comfortable for us in the garden. Your mother quite agrees," she added.

Already she was on her way downstairs. Probably she wanted to avoid his questions, or perhaps it was that she feared to see upon his face a look which might have terrified her.

1 3

HE WAS SEATED at the table, facing his mother.

"Evening's drawing in already," she grumbled. "Better light the lamp."

He asked her no questions, knowing that she would elude them. He would just let her run on, ready to catch in the torrent of her talk the first revealing words.

"Poor Madame Dubernet! Folks always used to say as how she was so proud—not as she hadn't every right to be, them being such an old family, and she owning so much land. If we was in her shoes I 'spect we should be just as proud, if not more. It's not everyone as'll lose by her death. Didn't Madame Agathe tell you? Not but what Madame isn't still alive, and it brings no luck a-burying folk afore they're dead. P'raps the good God'll still take a fancy to me first, after all. But doctor Salone's sure as how she's far gone. It'd be unnatural like for Madame Agathe to feel all that put about . . ."

Nicolas asked whether Madame Dubernet had "mentioned Agathe in her will."

"No, no," said the old woman: "nothing of that sort . . ."

"I don't understand you, mamma: I've no idea what you're talking about."

"There ain't nothing difficult *to* understand. It seems as they've decided, even if she do get well, to settle all old Camblanes' debts. No one won't have any hold any more on Belmonte, but it's all to be done on condition as the old man gives his property to his daughter, and renounces his rights. What d'you say to that, m'lad? But it's from Madame Dubernet, alive or dead, as Agathe is to have the princely gift, and not noways from old Armand."

"What difference does that make to me?" asked Nicolas wearily.

"*Hé bé*—this difference, that no one'll have the right to jabber. It's important for you that there shan't be no jabbering. Folk are so sharp-natured. Not but what it's common knowledge in Dorthe as the main of their fortune comes from Julia, from the Donzac side . . . But there you are in your dreams again, and not hark'ning to a word I say!"

So Agathe was not poor, as he had been led to suppose. Not a word of all this had she said to him. She had been keeping it in reserve to dazzle and defeat his old mother.

Madame Plassac was now well embarked on a tide of words.

"Last year old Camblanes had something of a seizure,

and all's going to ruin up at Belmonte. They'll be needing somebody to keep an eye on the place . . . Two years' grapes there are in store, enough to keep the vineyards in good heart. Livin's easy on the land. Well nigh a hundred hectares they've got, and just for one owner. So, Madame Agathe's been a-thinking of me . . . But you'll be asking by what right I should go and settle my old bones there—well, it do in great part depend on you . . ."

She got up and gave him a kiss.

"Ah! my little slyboots!" she exclaimed with a knowing look. "Folks may well say as the innocent don't go empty-handed!"

The Angelus was ringing from the Cathedral—unless it was the sacring bell, for, of course, it was the first Friday in September. Very soon now sleep would envelop this little half-dead town, which, in the course of centuries had been a Bishop's see, a prosperous city, and, during the wars of Guyenne, the scene of many battles whose very names are now forgotten.

His mother said: "Come with me, lad. There's something as I'd like to give you."

He followed her into the kitchen. She took a bundle of keys from her apron pocket, and opened the door of the linen cupboard.

"Hold the lamp," she said. "Ah, I'm too short. Give me that stool . . . I'm nothing but a bag of old bones."

She felt about and brought a cardboard box from under a pile of sheets.

"Take a look at *that.*"

She had often shown him the ring before, a garnet set in tiny brilliants—at least, she had always told him they were brilliants. This piece of jewelry had belonged to her father's sister, who had been cook to the Arbibats. Why had she been left it? "That I can't rightly say, lad."

He remained standing in the middle of the kitchen. It was as neat as a new pin. Everything was in its place. The lamp which he was still holding shone on the copper pots, making them gleam like round and rubicund cheeks.

"What do you want me to do with this ring?"

"Oh, the little caution, who'd a-thought it to look at him! This very night, in the garden, you'll find a finger to slip it on . . . See as you don't lose it. Aren't you going to thank your old mother for it?"

No, not a word of thanks did he give her. All the same, he had taken the ring, and was holding it clasped in his clenched fist.

14

"WHY did you tell me you were poor?"

"But I am poor, Nicolas. When we're living in Paris we shan't get a penny from Belmonte. The vines eat up everything. If we were living there we could make do, perhaps, but once we're settled in Paris . . ."

For a whole hour they had been sitting under the lime tree, and Galigaï had spent all that time trying to make it clear that she had not meant to deceive him. With one hand he was turning the ring over and over in the pocket of his jacket. She knew he had it.

"I don't mean to say that your mother won't send us food hampers. In the matter of eating we shall be helped out when they kill a pig, and, now and again, a chicken."

"I'd rather stick to the heated-up noodles and the spirit-lamp."

"So would I, darling." She kept her voice low, because she knew how irritated it made him to be called "darling." She had completely missed the irony in his words.

In the half darkness he could see the ugliness of his mother's garden. It was the one corner he had never succeeded in transforming. He hated the dusty lawn from which the fowls had scratched every vestige of grass, and the rabbit hutches which filled the night with their stench, even in June when the lime was in flower. No part of Galigaï's tormented brooding was hidden from him. At any moment now he might speak the word which would fill her cup of happiness to overflowing, or plunge her into the pit. . . . To bring life to a being who is dying of love . . . That temptation had more power over Nicolas this evening than had the wish to ensure the good officies of an accomplice whom Gilles needed. It was in his power to use the magic of those who are beloved. One word from him and the blood would flow back into the uncomely face which now was hidden from him by the darkness. He had not touched it, yet knew that it was wet with tears. He could not bear the sight of others crying.

"Don't," he said: "give me your hand.'"

She felt him slip the ring on her third finger. It was still warm from having been held so long within his palm. A wave of happiness and desire rose in her, but she knew that if she surrendered to the impulse, and allowed herself to be swept into his arms, he would repulse her. She forced herself to close the floodgates and bolt them strongly; to drive back the mad urgency within herself. She got up and pressed her lips to his forehead.

He said: "I have very little to give you. For that I ask

your pardon in advance. You mustn't expect too much of me."

"All I expect is the happiness of living close to you, within your shadow. After all, I am older than you. If you wish it, I will be an elder sister."

"You will need much patience," he went on. "It takes me a long time to get used to people. Sometimes, I never do . . . there's something inside me . . . I can't explain . . . do you remember the words of our risen Lord—'Touch me not . . .' . . . Can you understand what I mean?"

Oh, yes—she understood. Very humbly she said: "I will be your sister for as long as you wish. I am used to waiting. To most women everything is given at once. They have only to be themselves. But I know that only by dint of long perseverance shall I succeed in making a place for myself in your life. But even I must know that one day, however far off, I shall find happiness."

"Happiness!" he said gloomily: "happiness—you are ambitious, Agathe . . . who of us all finds happiness?"

She pressed her face to his shoulder, choking back her sobs. He pressed his lips—not, this time, to her eyes, but on her poor, thin hair, and drew her slightly to him.

"How good you are," she sighed.

Yes, to her undoing, he was good.

1 5

NEXT DAY she joined the Dubernets. Gilles, too, was off—"for the opening of the shooting season at Baluze"—he said to Nicolas. But he was lying, and knew that Nicolas was not deceived. Beyond the shadow of a doubt he was going to ensconce himself in some Bordeaux hotel. Marie would not be held a prisoner for the whole of every day in the nursing home. Galigaï's first letter confirmed his friend's suspicions. The girl had taken to going off for hours at a time.

Julia Dubernet's case was hopeless. There could be no question of moving her back to her own home. But the end might be long in coming. Agathe could not leave the dying woman for a moment, and every written word she sent to Nicolas was a lover's cry of impatience, almost of despair.

It was this note of despair that led him to hope that she might not be able to return to Dorthe before the end of the holidays. Nobody in the world could have blessed more fervently than he did this dilatoriness of death which was giving Julia Dubernet a breathing-space. Because of her long-drawn-out, her interminable, dissolution he would be able to get back to Paris without having to see Galigaï again. He refused to look beyond the vague promise of their engagement. It was enough that he must receive the daily letter which he would have delayed to open had it not been that he hoped each time to find his hopes confirmed. "No change." Those two words were always the first that leapt out at him from the page: "no change"—so he could breathe again. He studied the calendar. Twenty days to go, eighteen—soon now the new term would be beginning.

But meanwhile he could see, there, in front of his eyes, how the seed sown by Galigaï in his mother's mind was growing and putting forth its shoots. Belmonte! she was actually to be the mistress of Belmonte!—with power over people and beasts. Not that she would insist on being served at meals. Not that she would play at being a great lady, for a lady she was not. But it is easier to keep an eye on things from the kitchen than the drawing room. Already she had found out how the land lay. Old Camblanes, since his stroke, saw nobody. He was entirely dependent on his daughter, and "his daughter will be *my* daughter-in-law. 'Tis to us she will owe her happiness. Because of *you* she'll have to watch her p's and q's—but only for so long as you and I see eye to eye. There must be no bickering atween you and I, my lad. Folk'll say we're in luck's way—but 'tis sad when the good things come one's way too late, when one's an old woman. But there's nothing wrong with me, I'm as strong as a horse. And there I'll have a chance of resting me old bones. It's time as I had things done for me."

This kind of talk from his mother, even more than Galigaï's letters, made Nicolas eager to take wing. Like a criminal hoping to find a safe hiding-place in the great city, he was obsessed by the thought of Paris. Once she had got a pen in her hand, the imprudent Galigaï lost all sense of reserve. She threw the floodgates wide open. With a blank page before her she forgot how necessary it was to keep a careful eye on what she wrote. Weak with hunger and thirst, she sat herself down to the table with a will. Every two or three days he sent her, in reply, a few brief words. They did not disappoint her, so used had she become to never receiving from him the least mark of tenderness. Once he was back in Paris, he would scatter this handful of manna once every week, and she would be contented. True, he had taken an oath not to be false to the promise he had made. All he asked was that she should wait a while until he had grown accustomed to the idea, had been broken into it. For all he knew, she might grow calmer, might, like himself, end by preferring a tranquil union, comradeship, something like a friendship between fellow-students. What he always thought of as "it" —because he could find no other word, would be accomplished in cold blood, without passion, in the darkness.

He thought of it quite detachedly, as of something like a blood-transfusion. Still fifteen days to go—ten days, and he would be free. Then, suddenly, the letter came, three scrawled lines. "All is over at last. I must wait to see her into her coffin, but the day after tomorrow I shall be in your arms." He was sitting in the kitchen with his bowl of coffee before him. His mother snatched the letter from his fingers. "So, it's come at last. I always knew it must happen, but now I can be easier in my mind." It was a mercy for everybody concerned. Did Nicolas really mean to go back to Paris? That would be very foolish. He could easily get leave to stay on in order to get married. It was important not to let matters drag.

He replied in a dead voice that he would think, that he would see. He got up and went out into a day of misty sunlight. He walked along the Castillon road, feeling that he had fallen into a trap. He was caught. Useless to struggle. The smell of rotting wood, of burning leaves, of grape-must, the twitter of departing thrushes, heard but not seen, all the things that, since his childhood, he had loved in late September, came to him now as through the barred window of a cell. If only death indeed were death! If it were in very truth that sleep which the Church promises in its prayers for the dying: *Requiescat in pace* —may he rest in peace; Give them eternal rest, Oh Lord . . . But that prayer of peace brought him no assurance.

There was the response: *Et lux perpetua luceat ei:* light
eternal, light and fire. He had wandered into the chestnut
copse where, in the old days, he and Gilles had gathered
mushrooms. Automatically, he scraped away the dead
leaves with his toe. He had come up against the solid de-
posit in himself of Christian faith. He did not believe he
could escape. He was cornered, surrounded; there was no
way out into nothingness.

He must be content to bear upon his back the load
which only his own hand had placed there. "Woe unto
you, for ye lade men with burdens grievous to be borne,
and ye yourselves touch not the burdens with one of your
fingers." Ah, how much rather should Our Lord, when
he uttered that anathema, have said: Woe upon them who
lay upon their own backs the cross that crushes them,
that is beyond their capacity to carry, that is not *their*
cross! How many are there who perish beneath the super-
human burden which they have so foolishly assumed! It
is so easy to speak the *words* of self-sacrifice, to bind one-
self with a promise. One must walk, then, till death with
a ball of iron chained to one's ankle. But the convict's ball
of iron has no power over the convict. Oh God!—this
woman would have a right to his heart and body, night
and day, till death, and beyond death, too! . . .

With what implacable determination had she broken
through every obstacle! Nicolas thought of his mother.

At first she had been so hostile, but Galigaï had sub-
jugated her, so that now he could not even think of slam-
ming in her face the gates of Paradise just as she was
about to enter in! He clenched his fists. Why, oh why,
had he done what he had done? Who was it had taken
him by the shoulders and pushed him forward? Gilles
. . . that same Gilles who, as things turned out, had at-
tained his ends without the help of Galigaï; that same
Gilles, with the agate eyes in a face of flint, that living
knot of bones and muscles moved by appetites which
must always be satisfied . . . But whose the fault? He
had always, he, Nicolas, had to have some idol before
which he could immolate himself. Well, then, immolated
he must be, poor, stupid victim.

Such was his nature. But these deep eddies of his sensi-
bility should not prevent him from seeking a way out by
one last act of sacrifice. Everything should be carried
through in accordance with Galigaï's wishes. Not until
the marriage had been celebrated—and, even, consum-
mated, not until his mother's settlement at Belmonte had
become an accomplished fact, would he escape from life.
It is easy to "fake" a suicide. He started to turn over in his
mind the type of accident of which he might be held to
have been a victim. He felt calmer. But the dull rancor
which he felt against Gilles could not be kept from pen-
etrating into his new-found peace. As he walked along
the autumnal road which they had so often trod together,

he remembered how, in their friendship, since its earliest days, he had always been the dupe. The late smoke of chimneys in this town of death in life thickened the mist that clung about the towering mass of the Cathedral.

1 6

HE WENT home by way of the Rampart Walk. Suddenly he heard a familiar voice calling to him, and looked up. Gilles was leaning from the window of his own room.

Somebody had brought him back from Bordeaux by car. He had had himself dropped at Nicolas's house, because he could not wait to see him and tell him everything . . . Of course he hadn't gone shooting at Baluze! The two weeks he had spent in Bordeaux had been marvelous—though horrible, too. Marie had found it impossible to breathe in the nursing home. Even her mother had insisted on her going out. They had met in the Public Gardens, down by the harbor, anywhere—except in his hotel room near the Saint-Jean Station. They had resisted that temptation for several days—because they knew that no sooner had they shut the door . . . all the same, it had happened. He had felt as badly about it as Marie, and when they had parted afterwards, they had both been thoroughly shamefaced—to have snatched at happiness like that, to have indulged in furtive embraces, while, all the time, in another room, her mother . . . still, happiness covers a multitude of sins . . . "because I simply have got to tell you that I had no feeling of being jaded and washed-out afterwards—for the first time in my life! D'you realize what that means? . . . each time it happens I'm just as much carried away, just as much on top of the world . . . it's as though it were always the first time . . . Marie finds it all so perfectly natural and simple . . . she never imagined it could be different . . . but that *I* can feel like that . . . you know me . . . what a discovery! what a miracle."

He had not yet looked at Nicolas. He was used to carrying on monologues, and their subject was seldom other that himself. Nicolas's silence was a familiar and necessary background. But to-day it wasn't quite the same sort of silence—he felt the difference obscurely, and stared down at his friend who was lying half stretched upon the bed with his face to the wall. He seized him by the hair with both hands, and forced him to raise his head. Then he understood.

"What's up?—it can't be because of Galigaï!—what, it is? . . . You're not going to tell me you feel bound? . . . Yes, of course I understood . . . the engagement was to be a real engagement, but indefinite, isn't that what you intended? It never occurred to me that you could possibly mean anything else. You can't have thought I was going to stand by and see you swallowed alive—and by her, by *that* horror! Have you thought what it'll be like? You only think about yourself, but what about her? It'll just be killing her by slow degrees! What's that?—she'll die without a doubt if you abandon her? Nonsense—she knows a trick worth two of that! Oh yes she does!—you needn't worry your head about her! If you marry her you'll merely be putting a spoke in her wheel—both of you'll lead a miserable life . . . whereas with old Dubernet, now that he's a widower . . . why, of *course!*— if it wasn't for you she'd marry him like a shot—why, you ass, it's the talk of the place; you must be the only person who knows nothing about it! I won't say anything's happened, anything serious, I mean, but there've been plenty of straws to show which way the wind's blowing. Marie's noticed it herself. So you thought that all this handing back of Belmonte was just an act of pure friendship? Your mother's just been leading you up the garden. It's not Julia Dubernet's money that's been involved. Oh, I know that the property was hers all right—came to her from the Donzac connection, but the capital's old Dubernet's. He's been raking in the shekels for twenty years and more, under pretense of being a Banker—why, he's bought up all the small shopkeepers in Dorthe. Belmonte's *his* gift, his *personal* gift, get me?—a token of his gratitude. No, it's not impossible that he should have taken a fancy to Galigaï. In the country, every woman gets her chance sooner of later . . . He never does a

thing without asking her advice . . . they're always con-
fabbing together. He tells her all about what he's been
reading in the *Revue des Deux Mondes* . . . she's his
standing assurance that he's not just a country bumpkin
. . . You've got a dam' good excuse, more than an excuse,
a *reason*. You've been thoroughly taken in. Your honor
is involved, I see that, but it's not too late! Look here—I'll
run you over tomorrow evening to Langon, in father's
car. In forty-eight hours you'll be in Paris, just about the
time that Galigaï, the family, and the corpse will be turning up in Dorthe. From Paris you can send her a letter—a
carefully worded letter. I'll hang about here, just to soften
the blow. Your mother?—yes, that certainly is a point,
but, hang it all, you can wangle something about business
to attend to before you get married—then you can write
a second letter, to her—surely you're not going to risk
spoiling everything just because of your mother? Don't
tell me you're going to sacrifice your whole life simply to
save her from being disappointed—besides, the Comte
de Camblanes would have shown her the door inside of a
week, you can take my word for that. My father's been
attending the old war-horse for the best part of a life-time,
and I can assure you he's not the sort of bloke to go shar-
ing his manger with anyone."

By this time Nicolas had been reduced to saying over
and over again—"so you think? . . . you really suppose?" . . . He was still putting up a show of resistance.

Gilles said: "Don't fuss; do as I tell you, and wash your hands of the whole business." Yes, that was it: wash his hands! He was beginning to breathe more freely. Light was coming back into the world. The sun was burning through the mist. He could never have stood up for himself. It was Gilles who was lifting the great stones off his chest, one by one.

Nevertheless, he still forced himself to put up a fight. He'd got a conscience. "Well, I haven't!" Gilles replied in much the same tone of voice as he had used when he told Galigaï that he had no heart.

Nicolas's conscience went on plaguing him until the hooter at the sawmill informed the good people of Dorthe that they could sit down to dinner, and the Sacristan that it was time to sound the Angelus . . . All that morning, Madame Plassac had been on the move. The old parrot was up and down the rungs of her cage all the time. Since she wore felt slippers it was impossible to hear her coming. But it did her no good to plaster her least bad ear to Nicolas' door. The most she could hear was Galigaï's name mentioned once or twice. She did not doubt for a moment that Gilles had come along to upset the apple-cart. Not that she blamed him. Worry had kept her awake all the previous night. She had lit her candle. What had enchanted her the evening before had now become a subject of torment. Her Nicolas in *that* spider's web? Besides, one could never be sure. She might be bored to death at

Belmonte, miserable, and then what would become of her? Was there any certainty that she could get her own house back? It had belonged to her husband's father, and had been left to Nicolas, together with a small income which he had always handed over to her. In his innocence he had ignored the fact that the little property constituted the whole of his inheritance. How did she know that Galigaï might not have designs on her house? But, no, that was nonsense: *she* would have Belmonte . . . The great thing was to keep a weather-eye open. "I'll have the training of her when she's my daughter-in-law." All things considered, what she'd got to do was to cut the ground from under that young Salone's feet. Old mother Plassac decided that her best course would be to summon Madame Agathe by telegram. She pondered for a long time the cheapest way of wording it: "Return urgent"— two words. She couldn't put it more shortly. What would the woman at the post office think? Well, she was a newcomer, and not yet much interested in Dorthe folk.

Late that afternoon Galigaï appeared at the kitchen door. Madame Plassac was "browning" onions.

"So soon?"

Agathe was clutching a black leather bag. There was a smudge of soot on her left cheek. Her hair was straggling from under the boy's beret which she wore in place of a hat. "Is he upstairs?" she asked. Yes, he was. She breathed more freely. She had been prepared for anything. She knew she was strong enough to stop any leak. As usual, old mother Plassac was floundering in a sea of words. He wasn't leaving until the following evening. Agathe had all the time she needed to put a stop to that. But what was there to bother about, after all?

"It's only a question of there and back."

"Is that what he told you?"

"He did and he didn't. He don't think he can get married without seeing his Professor. There's leave to be got, and there's papers to be signed . . . and a mort of matters to be seen to."

"Is that the excuse he gave you?"

"Maybe yes, maybe no: maybe I found out for meself. You're behaving in a mighty strange way, Madame Agathe."

"I want to know, and I'm going to know!"

"You want! . . . you always thinks as it's enough to want things, Madame Agathe!"

She had turned to sweeping out her kitchen, and spoke now without raising her eyes.

"It isn't enough to want—it's being able as matters."

In a rather over-sweet voice Galigaï said: "Meaning by that . . . ?"

"Meaning just nothing at all, Madame Agathe. Why are you looking at me like that, seeing as no eggs is broken? But I do know my Nicolas: I'm his mother, ain't

I? There's not a sweeter-natured boy nowhere, but he can dig his toes in, too."

Galigaï lost her temper: "I don't need you to teach me about Nicolas!" she said. "Is he alone?"

"Eh, that he is—packing his things. And looking ahead, that's what he's doing. Taking every stick with 'im. Looks like he don't mean to come back," she added with a touch of malice.

Madame Agathe was already half way up the stairs. Old Madame Plassac stopped sweeping, and stood for a moment facing the open door.

"A horse can be led to the water," she remarked, "but no one can't make 'un drink, my fine madam!"

She listened to the sounds above her head in Nicolas's room; a chair being moved, a trunk being dragged across the floor. She could hear an exchange of words, broken by silences. She strained her ears, her head on one side, like a hen.

1 7

I CAME back to see to the funeral arrangements," said Galigaï. "There's going to be a terrific crowd—everyone for miles around. You didn't mention anything to me about going away."

Nicolas was standing in front of his yawning trunk. He felt ashamed of his fear, and ashamed at being caught like a child doing something it shouldn't.

"I've got business to attend to in Paris."

"When do you expect to be back?"

In just such a tone must she question Marie. She was the sort of governess who could never treat things lightly. He gave his reply with hanging head.

"In a week's time."

Galigaï pointed an accusing finger at the underclothing laid out on the bed, the suits, the books.

"I am still a free man, aren't I?" he said.

"Why not be frank with me?" her voice was dry. He caught his breath. He had fallen head over ears into the trap, but the trap had shown an unexpected chink. He looked up.

"All right!—if you must have it, I'm off!"

"What has been happening in my absence? Something must have happened—what was it?"

She was close to him, fixing him with her slightly protuberant eye. It had no lashes. He turned away.

"You've come straight from the train," he said. "Wouldn't you like a wash?"

Taken aback, she went across to the mirror. She shrugged: "Is that what's worrying you?"

"I have plenty more to worry me. For instance, what's this about the Dubernets making you a present? . . . I suppose you know what people in Dorthe are saying?"

"About Armand Dubernet and me?"

She felt re-assured: she smiled. He protested.

"Not that I believe it—you needn't think I do. You and Armand Dubernet"—he gave a shrug—"you'd never have dreamed of such a thing—I'm not quite a fool, you know."

"So that's it!"

The poor simpleton—thus to destroy his own defenses! He tried in vain to go back on what he had said: "Still, that *is* the gossip, and what should *I* look like? After all, my word is pledged." How miserable he looked. She felt as though a load had fallen from her. "So that's it," she said again. She felt relaxed, happy. "What a little silly you are, darling!" She made an awkward gesture as though to embrace him, but he slipped free. Forgiving now, and almost roguish, she gave him a gentle slap.

"You give up at the first check! . . . you poor sweet. Fortunately I've got strength of mind for two. So you thought I wouldn't be able to give up Belmonte for your sake? Well, I forgive you. I don't hold it against you!" Nothing he could do would make her loosen her hold. All hope, he felt, was gone. She wrinkled her nose, she exposed her teeth: never had she smiled so long at a time. In a gesture of compassion she held out her two hands to him, open, with her arms away from her body, like those of a plaster statuette of the Virgin. But he did not take them.

"Of course you didn't believe a word of it! All the same, you were frightened of what people were saying . . . No, don't interrupt me . . . I want to make it quite clear that nobody matters to me, nobody exists for me, but you. I shall refuse the Dubernets' generous offer. That's all over and done with. Don't think any more about it. That obstacle at least I have broken down!"

Did she really think she had broken it down? Of course she did! She was convinced that she had won.

"You must be mad!" he spluttered. "How could I possibly consent to such a sacrifice, especially when I have got nothing to offer in exchange—nothing, do you realize that—nothing at all?"

She pretended to think that he was talking about money, about possessions.

"But what you call nothing is, for me, everything. Don't you see that the only thing that exists in the world is you and me?"

Still smiling, she took a step toward him, her hands once more outstretched. The tentacles of an octopus could not have terrified him more. If only he could have cut them off at a blow, before they reached him!

"I have been lying to you, Agathe—that was just my excuse for escaping from something that terrifies me."

He had blurted it out in spite of himself, and began to feel easier. He had dealt her the fatal blow at last. She let her hands fall to her sides. She felt for the black leather bag which she had put on a chair when she came in, took a handkerchief from it, wiped her face, and fronted him again. She would isolate the obstacle, would assume that it consisted only of the fear he felt for the idea of the physical act. It was something that all adolescents felt, something that involved for them the whole female sex. It wasn't she in particular who had aroused it, not Agathe de Camblanes. She proceeded quite calmly with her explanation.

"This horror you speak about, Nicolas. Don't forget that you didn't make any bones about it on that evening in the garden when we got engaged. You even quoted the words of Our Lord—'Touch me not!' I replied that I perfectly understood, that you had nothing to fear, that I expected nothing, that I should ask only to be allowed to live in your shadow, to serve you. And then, you slipped this ring on my finger."

Her voice had become humble, urgent, persuasive. She held up her hand to show him the ring. She felt sure she could convince him that nothing new had occurred behind which he could hide. And nothing had. Her triumph was already complete. He could think of nothing to say. She went on, still humble, still insistent.

"Simply to serve you, nothing more than that, I swear it."

"Really nothing more?" He, who never laughed but sometimes smiled, burst into a guffaw.

"Nothing more? But that is exactly what I meant when I spoke of horror . . ."

Then, in a lower voice, he added: "I didn't mean 'it,' the unthinkable 'it.' It never occurred to me that that could be in question between us, tomorrow or ever." A note of rage had crept into his voice.

How terrifying it is when the sweet-natured grow angry! She had never before experienced this roughness in him. All of a sudden he had given vent to a deep-buried hatred.

"Even if I didn't come near you, even if I didn't touch

you, the idea of living with you every day and every night as long as I lived, would be impossible. I would rather die!"

She uttered a sharp groan, but it was clear that she had not caught the full meaning of what he was saying.

"No, please," she begged, "don't say that I have lost you!"

He was quite beyond himself.

"Of course you haven't lost me," he shouted. "How could you lose what you have never possessed! Vast spaces and great chasms have always stood between us!"

He was hitting out at random and he must go on hitting.

"Leave me something," she implored. "Leave me the memory of that night on the Castillon road, by the banks of the Leyrot."

Never, never would she loosen her hold. But he was relentless. "You had better know the truth. Never in all my life have I felt so far removed from you as I did then. It was as though there were infinite distances between us."

She looked as though she had received a mortal blow. Her arms hung down at her sides.

"Why, then, did you consent, why did you promise?"

She could not go on. It would have been easy for Nicolas, at that moment, to finish her off. He felt like a murderer. He was holding a throat in his grasp. He loosened his grip.

"Agathe!" he cried. "This is horrible!" He gazed with terror at the unrecognizable creature before him.

"My words ran away with me. There is no truth in anything I have been saying."

He laid his arm round her thin shoulders, and ever so faintly pressed her to him. She gave a hiccup. He went on.

"I have been clumsy, I know: but you must realize that I have been fighting on your side."

Up to that moment she had been as though half dead, but now she broke from him in a sudden access of rage.

"You're not going to tell me that what's going on, now, in this room, is for my good!"

He took her face between his hands.

"Look at me! I insist on your looking at me! I should have brought you infinite unhappiness. We should have been, you and I, each other's executioner. Am I right, or am I wrong?"

She groaned.

"If that were so, why did you have to wait until to-day to realize it?"

"It is late in the day, I know, but not too late, thank God!—not too late for you to build your life anew."

Once more he was holding her by the shoulders, and looking into her eyes. But she turned away her face. Fortunately she had not realized that he was referring to Armand Dubernet.

"A life without you?"

She was crying now, shedding great scalding tears. Her face was contorted. Moved perhaps by pity or by shame, he could not look at it. He felt faintly touched. He took her hand, made her sit on the bed, sat down beside her, and spoke almost into her ear.

"I am not without some sort of excuse, Agathe. I plead guilty, but all the same, I plead. You must try to understand. I have been the victim of that terrible strength of will which you possess, that strength of will which hurls you against every obstacle with a blind, an almost animal, obstinacy. You shouldered aside my poor defenses, without noticing that they closed again behind you. Isn't that true?"

"Yes," she said humbly, passionately; "I understand, I see my fault."

He consented to modify his sentence. Nothing was lost. It was not too late for him to become another person.

"I will reform, I swear it. I will vanish. You will never see me again, never hear me again, but, all the same, I shall be there."

Oh God! the corpse was showing signs of life! He moved away from her.

"It's all over!" he cried in a tone of exasperation. "Agathe, you must realize that it is all over!"

He drove home his point, he pressed upon the sword.

"What can I do, what say, to make you see that it is all

over? I have fought too long, I beg you to forgive me. Yes, it is for you to forgive me for having tried all this time to stand out against my feeling of disgust . . ."

At that she stiffened. Tight-lipped and dry-eyed, she took a step toward him, and hissed almost into his face.

"So, I disgust you, do I? But what woman wouldn't?"

So, at last it had come to that! She was drowning him in filth!—that at least was proof that she knew herself to have failed. Very calmly he replied: "If I am what you think I am, you have only too good a reason to rejoice that you are rid of me."

He went to the window. Down in the garden his mother was pretending to be busy with the washing. He did not turn his head when Galigaï approached.

"The swine who has made use of you won't get what he wants. That Salone of yours shall never have his Marie."

"Is that what you think?" he asked, unmoved.

She said: "You'll see . . ." and sat down on a chair, once more scrabbling in the bag for her handkerchief. He waited. This really was the end. She spoke again.

"Don't worry: I'm going."

Nicolas returned to the window. His mother was no longer in the garden. He stood staring at the lime tree. When he turned again, Agathe would have left the room. She gazed with a concentration of attention at the heavy profile, at the body which would thicken after its thirtieth year. At last she got up, went toward the door, seemed to hesitate.

"I suppose it doesn't occur to you to wonder what I am going to do when I leave here?"

He leaned his elbows on the sill. She could see only his back. She spoke again: "You're not afraid that I might kill myself?"

He did not turn his head. He had become blind and dumb. He made no movement until he felt convinced that she was no longer there. Then, he took out his handkerchief and wiped his hands. He did not pick up the ring which she had flung down on the floor. Standing in front of the mirror he stared at the man he really was.

1 8

THE funeral feast should have ended in a discreet glow
of well-being. Not that there had been anything very special about the food. It had been quite a simple meal—still,
the people of Dorthe know how to do themselves well:
paté of hare, a dish of haricot mutton. As the cousin from
Castillon said, "What mutton! Dorthe's the only place I
know where mutton isn't over-cooked!" All the same,
there was an air of gloom. What kept the guests from
really enjoying themselves was the sight of Madame
Agathe presiding at the head of the table (she had been
charged by the members of the family to represent them),
like a statue of grief. If the funeral ceremony had revealed one fact more than another it was that the dead
woman had been deeply loved by Madame Agathe. Her
despair was plain to all eyes. The people of Dorthe were
not quite sure whether most to admire Julia Dubernet's success in inspiring so much affection, or Madame
Agathe's power to feel it . . . How true it was that no
one should ever judge others! The salt tears seemed to
have acted upon Madame Agathe's eyelids like some cor-

rosive acid, though, at the best of times, they were in a permanently reddened state as the result of an incurable skin-irritation. "All the same," remarked the lady who was sitting next to the cousin from Castillon, "what a prospect this sad occasion opens up to her! Armand is fond of her, that's the long and the short of it! There is always a big prize in the lottery of life waiting for even the least attractive of women. All my cooks, at one time or another, have left me for the sake of some man—even the fat ones, the rheumy-eyed and the drunkards. That's how life is! Maybe Madame Agathe is going to see her dreams come true, and Armand won't get the worst of the bargain, either! He is used to her, and he needs someone in his house. After all, she has been running things in this family for years, and the only difference will be that he won't have to pay her! Not too bad an arrangement for him. Besides, do you realize that, should he outlive old Camblanes, Belmonte in the long run will come to *him?* Still, the dream is *her* dream . . . The more one thinks about it, the harder it seems to account for Madame Agathe's look of tragedy queen. I wonder if there is something going on that we know nothing about?"

This can have been no new matter of wonder to the good lady, because, after emptying her glass, and very slowly wiping her lips, she whispered into the ear of the Castillon cousin, "What *is* this secret of hers?" To which question the Castillon cousin, in the same low tone, and with difficulty restraining a laugh, replied, "Perhaps it's remorse. She may have poisoned her!"

"You shouldn't joke about such things!" said the lady, "just look at her, she hasn't swallowed a mouthful. I can't help wondering whether Armand and Marie feel it all as much as she does."

In his room upstairs, whence he could hear the murmur of voices and the subdued clatter of forks and dishes, Armand Dubernet was seated in front of a number of open drawers, filing away papers. There is nothing like a death to make a man turn to and put his affairs in order. "Now what," he wondered, "have I done with that contract?" Not for a long time had he been so mentally active. Marie, settled in a low chair, was acutely conscious of the delicious discomfort caused her by the letter she had slipped between her breasts. There was no necessity for her to read it again, for she had it all by heart. "I should perhaps have waited a little longer before rescuing that poor fly, Nicolas . . . Still, the spider's no longer got her web, and when a spider's without a web the sooner one crushes her underfoot the better. All the same, you'd better go carefully with Galigaï. Quite apart from her, though, we really oughtn't to revel quite so much in our happiness for the next day or two. We do owe that amount of consideration to your poor mother, though how I am going to stand not seeing you for so long I do *not* know. Of course, there's no reason why we shouldn't meet—provided we behave sensibly—but I'm hanged if I know which of us is the weaker, you or I, when it comes to being sensible. We can't be together three minutes without . . . Look here, I've got a notion . . . Come out after dinner—not to our usual place under the terrace wall, by the tulip-tree, but to the Leyrot, just where they've been cutting the alders. You needn't make a secret of where you're going, only you'd better wrap up well. I shall be on the further bank, I'll light a bit of a fire to show you where I am, but I shall see your cigarette in any case . . . Put on that white woolen coat you bought at Luchon . . ."

"I think you should have a talk with Madame Agathe, my dear, about what clothes of your poor mother's you want to keep. We'll send along the rest to the orphanage . . . You're not listening to a word I say, Marie . . ." added Armand with a sudden show of impatience.

"There's nothing I want to keep." She was thinking of all the scalloped under-bodices, of the fantastic drawers, of the petticoats which her mother used to attach to her stays.

"No doubt Madame Agathe will find them come in very useful," she said with a wicked glint in her eye.

"Why Madame Agathe more than you?"

He stopped short. Galigaï had just entered the room

without knocking. Marie was only too well aware why the woman was looking like a ghost fresh from the grave. But what was Armand thinking?

"I could not endure it a moment longer," said Madame Agathe. "There is something I wish to discuss with your father. Would you mind leaving us for a few moments, Marie?"

"Why should I? Can't you say what you have to say in front of me? Surely, to-day of all days, my place is with my father?"

"Marie, don't be impertinent!" said Monsieur Dubernet.

All the same, he dared not order her from the room. Madame Agathe had shown no reaction whatever to the girl's words. With a perfectly expressionless face she sat herself down beside him to help him with the sorting of poor Julia's bills. Marie had not stirred from her low chair. She sat very upright, with her legs pressed close together. She had been worked up into a condition of mistrustful watchfulness by the paper which she had hidden between her breasts. It tickled; actually, it rather hurt.

From below there came a rising sound of voices, a sudden burst of laughter quickly suppressed. Somebody was speaking. It was Monsieur Borot, a Member of the General Council, and he was revealing to his horrified relations the sad fact that Dorthe was about to lose its position of a "Sous-Préfecture." André Donzac, a seminarist of nineteen, and a nephew of Julia's, a precocious young gentleman, whose insolence was a by-word in Dorthe, and who had at first been silent (out of fear that he might be put to sit next the Canon), had found his tongue after the meat course. He enquired rather loudly whether the decline of Dorthe as a community was an isolated phenomenon—whether, in fact, the township had become a dead cell, comparable to those patches of callused skin which occasionally appear on human feet, or whether, on the contrary, it was itself a center of infection, an example of the mortal sickness to which the whole country, perhaps the whole of Europe, was succumbing. Was the question one of a rotting limb or a piece of strictly limited dead skin?—"that's what I should like you to tell me, sir."

Armand, Agathe, and Marie could hear the raised voices, the scrape of chairs, and then, silence. Marie never took her eyes from Galigaï's face. It was not so much that she wanted to watch her, as that she felt she must not show any sign of weakness. She was struggling against a sense of power, of triumph. She was overcome by a feeling of shame, and was trying to pray for that dead mother who had never liked Gilles—who might, indeed, have hated him, and, in the long run, come between them . . . What hateful thoughts!—if only God would not punish her for entertaining them! "Oh, please, God—no: I really am terribly upset that poor mamma is dead. You who know all must know that I loved her." She forced herself to remember the days when she could not bear to be away from her mother, even for an hour, and how Madame Dubernet had always complained that "the child is forever clinging to my apron-strings." It used to be a commonplace that she "has no feeling for anyone but her mother" . . . Mamma, nailed down in that box, her hands bound together by the rosary, her chin supported by the tight bandage which the dead wear . . . Gilles! of the unkind face—unkind to others, capable of softness only to her, with hard, dark eyes cut from some resistant stone, which grew veiled and misted when he looked at her. One night she had even tasted a tear in them. He had told her that he never cried. "If I am crying now," he had said, "it is because I love you so much." Those had been his very words. She had not dreamed them. "I am crying because I love you so."

19

HADN'T it occurred to you that she is probably with him at this very moment?"

Armand Dubernet shook his head, but she would not let the subject rest.

"Where do you think she is, then?"

His shrug expressed ignorance.

"Certainly not with him: it is unthinkable that she should behave so on the very evening of her mother's funeral."

Armand Dubernet and Madame Agathe were "finishing off" the cold mutton like a married couple of long standing. Marie had refused to come to dinner. Not a word had been exchanged until the end of the meal. Madame Agathe was folding her napkin.

"Come out on the terrace with me; I am quite sure we shall find them under the tulip-tree."

Armand Dubernet drank a last glass of wine, and struggled to his feet with considerable effort.

"Certainly not," he said. "I should prefer not to know."

"If I come back and tell you I have caught them, will you believe me then?"

Not a word did he answer, but led the way to the drawing room. It was, he said, a warm night, and he was sorry that they could not have the shutters open, but it would not be seemly so soon after the funeral. He was talking for no better reason than to avoid a silence. He must, thought Agathe, long ago have guessed her secret, for, do what she might, she could not keep the adored name out of her conversation. Of course he knew all about that wretched little usher, the son of the old woman who looked after the Cathedral chairs, realized the indelible mark that he had left upon this noble, ardent creature, whose scent he had so often picked up at the end of the corridor, from behind her closed door. He followed her now with heavy tread into the entrance-hall. She took down a cloak and threw it round her shoulders. Then she turned to him, urgent, insistent.

"Yes or no, will you believe me if I tell you that I have caught them?"

Once more he made no answer. She slammed the glass door behind her, and plunged into the darkness of the garden.

He had been right—it was warm. The white gravel of the path leading down to the terrace looked like an earthly continuation of the Milky Way. It was as though beneath the throbbing night-sky, a flowing tide had once more lifted the old grounded vessel. The Cathedral appeared to be floating above the roofs and the mist. She could feel in her flesh what such a night must mean to the two young creatures pressing together under the tulip-tree, the two young creatures whose happiness she was about to sully. Her despair drew nourishment from the ecstasy with which the darkness must be rich for those twin lovers now so close to her, barely a stone's-throw away. Perhaps they had not heard her steps upon the path, though even if they had the charm which held them there fast bound would have been proof against fear. Why, oh why, had she come out? Why had she not stayed indoors under the concentrated glare of the ceiling-light, in that gloomy dining room, with an old man sunk in seeming lethargy, and secretly longing to touch her? What had she, in her wretchedness, to do with this night which Marie and Gilles would, perhaps, remember, when death should come for them and bless God because he had granted them a moment such as this? Once again she yielded to the instinct which had always driven her on, head down, to meet every obstacle in her path. But it deceived her no longer. She reached the great tulip-tree. A gentle breeze was stirring the leaves above her head. It was as though the night were breathing. There was no one there. The grass looked bruised and flattened in their secret spot, but they must, this evening, have found some other hiding place.

"Are you looking for me, Madame Agathe?"
The mocking voice was Marie's.
"Can't you see me? I can make out your figure quite clearly on the terrace. I am over here, by the felled alders."
Better for Galigaï if she had turned tail and fled. But no, she must see, must touch this happiness of others.
"Here . . . I am sitting on one of the stumps."
The girl was, indeed, alone, motionless in the darkness, a little doe, spreading her scent upon the wandering breeze to bring the hare to her.
"I'll make room for you beside me."
"There's a chill striking up from the Leyrot," said Madame Agathe: "you'll catch your death of cold."
"No, that fire is keeping me warm."
"Fire?—what fire?"
"There, on the other bank."
Listlessly, Galigaï looked at the flickering flames, dying down until they were almost extinguished, then leaping up again.
"A fire so far away brings me no sense of warmth. It is your heat, Marie, beside me that I feel."
The animal glow of the young body pressed to hers was intolerable. Marie said nothing. She was no more

than a child, and, as a child might, was amusing herself with making an arabesque of signs upon the darkness with the lighted end of her cigarette. Then, Galigaï understood. A burning branch was being shaken on the further bank. She could not see the young man, but knew that he was there, flaming more brightly than the torch he was waving above his head. A sudden leaping plume of fire revealed him for a moment, standing with thin legs apart. He stretched his arms. Then, the darkness swallowed him.

Yes, Galigaï had understood. The lovers had willed it that a sword should separate them, a liquid blade murmuring among the reeds and chattering over the stones. Never so intermingled would they be as on this evening, never would feel themselves to be so wholly one with the plants of the earth and the stars of the heavens, with the uncreated Being, and their own forefathers now laid to rest. Marie heard the branches crackle and crash before the onset of some animal in flight. Galigaï was no longer there.

When she re-entered the drawing room, Armand Dubernet was just where she had left him, but he had lit a cigar. Of what was he thinking, sitting there enveloped in ill-smelling smoke that coiled from nose and mouth? He did not look up. His heavy, creased eyelids never so much as moved. He knew that, at this precise moment, he must not look at Madame Agathe. Would he very much mind, she asked, if she went straight to her room. The truth was, she felt completely exhausted.

"Did you see Marie?"

With a movement of the head she admitted that she had.

"Was she alone?"

For a few seconds Galigaï hesitated. If she gave a true report of what she had found, it would redound to the young people's credit. She heard herself say, "Yes and no." He did not press the point. When he spoke again his voice was low.

"It seems to me that we have reached a stage . . ."

She turned to face him, her hand already on the latch.

"You don't, I hope, mean that you're thinking of giving way?"

He said nothing, and she went on to ask whether it wouldn't be more decent to wait until the earth had hardened over Julia's grave. He made a movement of the head.

"Ah, poor Julia, dear Julia . . . what can it matter to her now? . . . The situation has got to be faced, you know. Only yesterday Dr. Salone said to me, with a very meaning look, 'the sooner the better, Monsieur Dubernet.'"

The governess raised her shoulders in a shrug which

clearly meant—Oh, we all know about Dr. Salone! But he would not be turned from his purpose.

"Dr. Salone is a man of very scrupulous feelings—there are not many in Dorthe of whom I'd say that—though doubtless there are others scattered about the world . . . You have too great a contempt for the human race, Agathe. There are times, you know, when we *must* have confidence in people."

Instinctively he broke off, as though in expectation of one of Julia's "charges of buckshot" which, in the old days, had always greeted that sort of remark. He could almost hear the sharp voice: "did you remember to take your shooting-coat to the cleaners?" But Julia had put away her gun for ever now. No power in all the world could stop Armand Dubernet from listening to the sound of his own voice. Hesitatingly he continued: "The sooner the better, don't you agree?"

Galigaï came back into the room: "Do I understand you to be talking about a marriage? . . . Do you really know anything at all about young Salone . . . Have you the vaguest idea what he is like?"

"Whatever he is like, Marie loves him . . . At that age all young men are alike. There's nothing to choose between them."

She lowered her voice till it was almost a whisper: "He is an *extremely* undesirable type . . . I happen to know a few things about him . . ."

135

"What sort of things?" he asked. Galigaï was leaning against the wall. She had lost all belief in her power to influence destiny, but was yielding, all the same, as it were, to the reflex action of her will.

"It is difficult to put into words—but the things I mean are . . . well, they're *disgusting*." Her voice seemed to express more of weariness than loathing.

"What things?" asked Monsieur Dubernet again. She passed her hand over her forehead, and said in a flat voice . . . "after all, I have no proof . . ." In that moment she reached the very nadir of her misery. The fat man in his cloud of smoke did not move. His rheumy eyes glittered under their wrinkled lids. There was something of the toad about his immobility. They could hear Marie stop for a moment outside the door. She pushed it half open, saw her governess, and at once closed it again. Galigaï listened to the sound of her light footsteps dying away.

"My usefulness here is at an end," she said. "I shall leave this week."

At that the toad stirred. He stood up on his short legs.

"You must be crazy, Agathe," he said.

"It is you who are crazy. If my pupil is getting married what possible justification is there for my staying?"

He dropped his cigar into the ash-tray, and lumbered toward her.

"This evening—the evening of the funeral—is no time to talk of what I have in mind. All the same, I feel quite certain that Julia would approve . . . in fact, that Julia hoped . . . You must know perfectly well what I mean. All I want you to realize just now is that your manner of life would not, in any way, be changed. You could, if that is your wish, keep on the room you have at present."

He turned slightly away, and, in a lower tone: "—I shall ask nothing of you," he went on: "I swear that I will not so much as lay a finger on you without first obtaining your consent. I will behave exactly as though I were your father—it is a habit that I have acquired."

She choked back a cry, the same cry as that which Nicolas had spat in her face: "You fill me with disgust!" She was, however, amazed to find that one part of herself did not say "no," was, in fact, already acquiescent. She would not have to face total defeat. The unrevealed disaster of her life would be seen by the people of Dorthe as a triumph. Even in Marie's presence she would be able to hold her head high. It was she who would remain in occupation of the battle-field. What a perspective of years stretched before her!—all a lifetime in which to lie heavy on the destiny of the girl who, to-night, had mocked her so abominably!

Monsieur Dubernet was counting the seconds. A whole minute had already slipped away, and she had made no protest.

"Forget everything we have just been saying, Agathe. There is no urgency for us. It is essential that you should think long and calmly about what I am proposing before reaching a decision. Marie will need you more than ever between now and the date of her marriage. You will have to see about her clothes, act as her chaperone . . . Happiness is not what people of your age think it is. Happiness is the knowledge that one is not dependent on others; happiness is the certainty that one occupies the leading position in the society one lives in; happiness . . ."

She interrupted him: "What in the world can I have been thinking about! . . . I have forgotten all about your tisane!"

Galigaï had picked up Julia's "gun."

When she had left the room Armand went back to the lamp and sat down again. He was thinking: was he too old, at fifty-eight, to get a son? He would consult Dr. Salone. But no, he must not ask too much of life. It was extremely improbable that he would ever have a son. But now, at this moment, he knew what was for him the most important truth. He would marry the heiress of Belmonte. He would possess Agathe, and Belmonte would be his.

2 O

EH, BUT I was sore tempted, though I didn't swallow the hook," said Madame Plassac, that same evening to her son. He was to start for Paris the next morning, and was sitting now beneath the ceiling light while she gave him his supper. She had taken the turn of events better than he had expected. That, at least, was some consolation.

"The very moment I saw that Madame Agathe come into my kitchen, I knew everything was coming crashing down, and yet it would all be for the best. Don't you think it a mighty strange thing that my eyes should've been suddenly opened? I must have been dead crazed to think I could have lived with her, and been at her mercy —to say nowt of the fact that a soft-natured creature like you would've been swallowed down whole in no more'n a week. Ah, you should've been strong—like some I could name. There's some women, true enough, as needs a man to hit 'em good and hard!"

"I hit her hard, all right!" he muttered, "a great deal harder than you have any idea!"—but he did not repeat the words loud enough for her to hear. This old woman who could see no farther than her nose (for all her spectacles), was his mother, and he was her son. Oh, he was sweet and soft enough to those who gave him a wide berth, who did not force him back on the last line of his defenses.

"She's pretty cut up now, I warrant, and dearly would I like to see her mug! I dursn't look too close when she was coming out of church. I'd have liked to see her eyes!"

She sat down facing him, and cut a piece of cheese. Very quietly he replied: "Her eyes will soon be dry—just as soon as she's become Madame Dubernet."

"Madame Dubernet, is that really where the wind lies? You may be right—but what an idea!"

She was clearly impressed.

"If Madame Agathe can bring *that* off, she'll have spunk, and none can say different . . . But what low-down trick will she play us, maybe?"

"What low-down trick should she play?" he asked wearily. "Believe me, it will all be for the best."

His rather coarse hands were lying motionless on the table before him. Yes, everything was for the best, Madame Plassac was thinking, with a vacant look in her eyes. She said: "In any case that Salone lad'll have an enemy on his doorstep, that is, if she don't stop the two from getting spliced."

Nicolas shook his head.

"No, it's too late to stop that now . . . but she'll have

all her life in which to pull their happiness to pieces."

"Now don't you go getting your finger pinched again."

"You can be easy on that score. I'm not getting mixed up in that kind of trouble."

He touched the letter in his pocket. Gilles had had it delivered to him in the course of the day. He had not learned it by heart as Marie had learned hers. Gilles asked to be excused from spending this last evening with him. They would be meeting again, soon, in Paris. He, Gilles, would have to go back there to fetch some clothes and books which he had left behind. Then, he would return to Dorthe at once. The wedding had been fixed for January. Marie and he had decided that they would live at Baluze.

Nicolas said in a low voice: "There is not much difference between men and insects."

"What's that?"

"Gilles and I have both emerged from the chrysalis."

"Always talking nonsense."

He got up. He wanted to go for a walk in the darkness. He asked his mother for the key.

"Must that Salone steal you from me, even on your last evening?"

"It's nothing like that," he said drily. "Gilles is with his girl. I only just want to get a breath of air."

If that was all she would wait up for him, as she always did.

insisted in the same, flat voice, "Give me the
j.

The old woman made a gesture of refusal with her
hand, and grinned, showing her gums. He knew that she
had made up her mind. He moved round the table, and,
without raising his voice, said: "Come, give me the key
—quickly, now!" She was so surprised that she stood bolt
upright, leaning against her chair.

"What's come over you," she mumbled. "That's no way
to behave. The key's mine . . ."

"Yours?—you seem to forget, mamma, that this is *my*
house . . ."

At that she sat down, and looked her son up and down:
"*Hé bé!*" she said, and then again, "*hé bé!*"

"Don't keep me waiting!"

"Now where can I have put that there key," she muttered.

"It's in the pocket of your apron."

She fumbled for a moment, and held it out to him with
a hand that trembled slightly. He almost snatched it
from her. She followed him into the passage.

"Give your old mother a kiss, then. True enough, you're
twenty-eight—quite a man."

The Castillon road, too, looked like an extension of the
Milky Way. He listened to the sound of his solitary footsteps, but felt no wish that Gilles were with him. He
walked on in loneliness. He was prey to a melancholy

142

hunger which all the kingdoms of the earth could not have satisfied. His only companion was a tenderness that now lay hidden from all eyes, a tenderness that lay outspread like the sea beneath the mindless stars. At a spot where a clearing in the pines showed a great expanse of sky, he stopped and turned his head. He saw the black bulk of the stranded Cathedral caught among the roofs. The human insects had, at least, reared high that ship, and built it to the measure of the love which had had some of them by the throat. He started to walk again and reached the place where the road crossed the Leyrot. He sat upon the parapet, a stranger to himself, detached from all his fellows. It was as though he had agreed with somebody to meet him there.

POSTSCRIPT TO

THE LOVED AND THE UNLOVED

NOW that *The Loved and the Unloved* is about to be published, I feel much the same anxiety as I did, thirty years ago, whenever one of my books appeared. I am afraid, not so much that I may shock, as disconcert, those of my readers who share with me a religious outlook. The misunderstanding to which I refer may arise in circumstances which have nothing to do with the publication of a novel. For instance, a member of one of the Religious Orders wrote to me that *La Table Ronde* had disappointed him. The fact that my name appeared at the head of the list of those responsible for its editorial policy, had decided him to read the periodical, and, no doubt, to recommend it to the young men in his charge. This Father thought it strange that I should devote so much time to so *useless* a production. This is an excellent example of the type of misunderstanding to which I have referred. For the member of a Religious Order, and even for a simple layman, provided he be sufficiently fervent, to write means to serve.

That the artist should have no concern beyond painting to the best of his ability, and placing what he has
painted—as André Gide has put it—in the best possible
light, is something that a man of apostolic calling finds it
more than usually difficult to understand.

There do, I need hardly point out, exist members of
Religious Orders who have given much thought to the
problems inherent in the act of literary creation. They
would most certainly admit that the novelist must be
constantly on his guard against trying to *prove* anything.
They realize that his duty is to make the most of his own
peculiar vision of human life and human persons. It re-
mains true, however, that if the world which the Christian novelist portrays is noticeably denuded of Grace,
that if God seems to be absent from it, the pious critic
has a perfect right to hold that the work in question may
fairly be used in evidence against its author.

As a result of having had, recently, to go through the
proofs of a Collected Edition of my works, I have been
compelled to re-read all of them, and it has been borne
in on me that though, quite often, Grace does "break in"
it has tended to do so less and less as I have grown older.
In *The Weakling* it makes an appearance only in the final
pages, and in *The Loved and the Unloved* the reader is
not told until the very last sentence, almost the very last
word, that one of my characters is moving toward God.
All the same, that "someone" waiting for Nicolas Plassac

where the road crosses the Leyrot *is* God. But before that meeting could take place I had first to destroy the idol—Gilles Salone. It was necessary that Nicolas should be detached from appearances, from his own false image of himself. Galigaï makes him realize that the lusts of the flesh are productive of intense unhappiness, that he is no less capable of cruelty than other men, and that he has never really loved anyone but God. The world I have described is the world as it appears to Nicolas when the scales fall from his eyes.

The picture I have painted is indeed black. It shows mankind as warped, as showing to the world a mask fixed in a hard and hateful grimace. It shows humanity untouched by Grace. In favor of whom, or of what, can such a portrait bear witness? That question sums up the critical attitude of the Christian. What I sought to express was precisely those shards and fragments of life as it is lived in a half dead provincial town, and from which Nicolas separates himself at God's call. When I started the book I did not know that this was my intention. The artist stresses this or that characteristic almost unconsciously, and in obedience to his creative instinct. He may even distort his material the better to give form and substance to those feelings of pity and horror which, since his earliest years, he has felt when confronted by certain persons and certain lives. To the over-life-size figures whom, as a sickly child, I saw, noted, and fixed in my mind, now, grown to maturity, and as an old man, I have given significance. The social prejudices and priorities obtaining among the "insects" of a country society, would be matter only for mockery and raillery, were it not for the fact that there, as elsewhere, there, perhaps, more than elsewhere, the secret drama of a sexual desire which is near neighbor to disgust, finds its free development.

I might well have called *The Loved and the Unloved* —*Desire and Disgust*. The subject of the book is one aspect of that hatred between the sexes which is rarely studied because, in the first place, it is something upon which we do not like to dwell, and because mutual love will always be a more pleasing spectacle to human beings so long as they continue to feel a need for love. I have not, in *The Loved and the Unloved* deprived the reader of that spectacle. The book is, among other things, the story of a happy pair of lovers. But, that the true theme may be made to stand out more clearly it does treat also of the repulsion felt by a young man pursued by an "amazon" who is convinced that, even in love, the force of sheer determination, of sheer will-power, can be made to triumph. That a young man, not naturally inclined to vice, should be satisfied with a feeling of friendship—or rather, of the emotion that falls half way between friendship and love —inspired in him by a childhood's companion, so completely as to let it absorb his whole capacity for sentimental devotion, is something that the reader of *The Loved and the Unloved* may find it hard to accept. He may be led to assume the worst of this Hippolytus who is without an Aricia.[1] But if he does so he will, in my opinion, be wrong.

But, to return to the main point at issue. My priestly correspondent will find here fresh reason to wonder what the results of my labors amount to, what good they will do, spiritually, to those who read them, and how I can reconcile so distorted a view of the human animal with the faith I claim to have in his vocation of sanctity. It would be easy for me to get out of the difficulty, by arguing as I have done on more than one occasion, during the last forty years. I might point out that evil is a reality in this world of ours, that the people I set out to paint are fallen creatures, tainted from birth, that I have done no more than provide a dramatic illustration of what a Bossuet and a Bourdeloue have already denounced, that no artist should force his talent, and that mine does not easily breathe the air of sublimity.

This is all perfectly true, but it does not really answer the objections put forward by the priest or the pious layman, both of whom will retort at once by saying that, even at the risk of forcing my talent, I ought to have devoted a final chapter to showing the victory of Grace in Nicolas. They cannot be expected, they will say, to take my word

[1] Aricia is a Princess of Athens to whom, in Racine's tragedy of "Phèdre," Hippolytus is married. (Translator.)

for its occurrence. It is one thing, they will declare, to denounce the vices of mankind from the pulpit in order to combat them, and quite another to display those vices, not, indeed, with the purpose of making them seem attractive, but at least of serving the purposes of a work of art which shall be judged as an end in itself. For there, in my opinion—leaving aside the Jansenist contention that all depicting of human passions is criminal—lies the real sin which no Christian artist can avoid who does not manifestly employ his gifts in the interests of his Faith. The work which is *merely* an end in itself becomes an idol, on whose altar the artist will sacrifice everything, even if that everything shall include, as with Proust it did, life itself. But, as I myself have often pleaded, the work of art is of service to mankind simply because it does not seek deliberately to "serve." Do I really believe that? Let me confess at once that the work of art tends much more frequently to distort than to instruct. For the creative writer to pretend that he helps us to an understanding of mankind by painting a picture in dark and extravagant colors, is sheer hypocrisy. Living persons are never like the characters of fiction. The people presented in novels or on the stage are a race apart. They in no way instruct us about ourselves, or, at least, not usefully, in the first place because these invented creatures are conditioned and circumstanced by the author, in the second, because, no matter how complex they may be, they inevitably express some tendency, some passion, or some vice, and are, to that extent, detached from the human context. We have most of us had experience of misers and hypocrites, but we have none of us ever met a Tartuffe, a Harpagon or a Grandet. There is a planet Balzac, a planet Dostoievsky, inhabited by monsters with the faces of men and women. They are just as much, perhaps more, alive and less ephemeral than the inhabitants of our planet Earth, but not in the least, except superficially, do they resemble them. When we say of some woman living in a country town, that she is "a Bovary," we are doing no more than comparing her with an abstract type in the interests of conversational convenience. We know perfectly well that between Madame Bovary and a creature of flesh and blood there is no true connection such as might be used to point a moral lesson.

And even when the artist goes out of his way to avoid the introduction of "types" and "characters," the colorless and insubstantial world into which he introduces us has little in common with our own. Admittedly, the elements which go to build it up are borrowed from reality. That is true of all novels of no matter what kind. The best as well as the worst are composed from details provided by recollection, fixed by memory, but retouched and rehashed for the purpose of presenting a "picture." There is no such thing as a novel which genuinely portrays the *indetermination* of human life as we know it.

The most, therefore, that may be conceded is that the novel, though it does not throw any revealing light on persons living in the actual world, may, and does, give us a great deal of information about the author. As something that increases our knowledge of human nature, and can therefore be used as a tool by the schoolmaster or the moralist, it may be useless. But it does furnish a considerable amount of evidence about the man who wrote it. But that is no very great achievement, and my Priest would be perfectly within his rights in judging that the interest to be derived from absorbing a certain amount of information about François Mauriac as a result of reading his novels, is insufficient compensation for the total uselessness of his works, to say nothing of their possible harmfulness to those among whom he is called upon to labor.

It follows, then, that the Christian who happens also to be a novelist must resign himself to pleading no better an excuse than that of "vocation." He writes novels because he has some reason to think that he was born into the world to write, seeing that from childhood on he has struggled endlessly to do so. He is in much the same position as a dancer of my acquaintance who, at the age of six, was already practising "entrechats" and "points," or, as my brother, the Abbé who, at the same age, compelled me to kneel in adoration before the altar which his childish hands had built. But, in saying this, I am only too well aware how rash it is to conclude that what seems, on all the evidence, to be our determined destiny, must necessarily be the expression of God's will. A vocation for evil, no less than a vocation for good, may well strike sparks from the young.

Still, it may be that I was created, and set down in one tiny segment of the Universe at a period when Revolt had become the theme on which most of our distinguished thinkers chose to expend their energies, for the sole purpose of bearing witness to Man's guilt when judged by the infinite innocence of God, and, as R. M. Albères said, in his review of *The Weakling*—"to set against a literature determined by metaphysics, in which man girds at everything, one based upon psychology, in which man girds only at himself."

François Mauriac.